SWEET

SWEET

Julie Burchill

YOUNG PICADOR

First published 2007 by Young Picador
an imprint of Pan Macmillan Limited
20 New Wharf Road, London N1 9RR
Basingstoke and Oxford
www.panmacmillan.com

Associated companies throughout the world

ISBN: 978-0-330-43911-4

3 5 7 9 8 6 4 2

A CIP catalogue record for this book is available from
the British Library.

Typeset by Intype Libra Ltd
Printed and bound in Great Britain by Mackays of Chatham plc, Kent

Thank you to Tom Gross, Ben Green, Noel Williams and the Barnabus Fund for their help in explaining to me the terrible plight of Christians in Pakistan.

Also thanks to Robert Caskie for being a firm pair of hands, Chilli Pete for his advice about chillis, Amy Raphael for her advice about babies, Chas Newkey-Burden for the names on the Pride floats and Sara Lawrence for fun in the sun and general debauchery.

This book is dedicated to its editor, Harriet Wilson — without whom it would be precisely 35 pages long.

1

When I got out of jail with a heroin habit and a fat arse, I really thought that things could only get better. Then I found out that my husband, Mark, the minger, had only run off and taken the baby with him! Not to mention my iPod. I mean, I can have another baby – but it took me two years to put my proper soundtrack together.

So I did what I've done since I was thirteen, whenever I needed to think about stuff – lifted a half-bottle of vodka, rolled a giant spliff and took it down to the beach. I was born in Brighton and I've lived here all my life, and sometimes it gets on my tits, but I've never got over the fact that you can sit on the beach and look at the sea all for free; doesn't matter how much money you earn, you get the same view.

I grew up way back from the seafront on the Ravendene Estate, in this totally pants tower block, whereas the rich Londoners who've been taking over this place for the past ten years now all buy themselves a cushy little sea view from their big white houses. But as I said, once you're down here on the beach, all that changes; you're all equal. For once.

After a bit I found a pen in my bag and made a list of things for and against me on the inside of an old Tampax tube.

AGAINST
Fat arse
Heroin habit
No money
Mark and baby gone

FOR
Total goddess from arse up
Heroin habit only sniffing, not shooting, so easily lost
Still only 17
Mark and baby gone

I thought then 'Dyke' and my pen hovered over both lists but in the end I didn't know if that was for or against, so I called it a day. Besides, how did I know I was one? I could've just had a soft spot – for that posh little cow Kim Lewis. My Kizza. Now swept away by her doting parents to a place where me and my evil ways would never find and corrupt her again, apparently. We'd see about that!

See, the way I look at it, me and Kim could have had one sweet life together, what with my brains and her looks. Or was it the other way around? I can never make my mind up, and I guess that when that happens, when you aren't sure who's got what, that's when you're really cooking. Anyway, plenty more fish under the bridge and all that; it's not like Brighton wasn't heaving with fit girls to perve over and steal off, if it came to that. And as for blokes, well we KNOW that they can't resist a little Sugar. So at the end of the day, it was prob'ly best not to decide yet if I was a dyke or not, but just to keep my options open, as it were.

I was getting well cold sitting on the beach, so I trudged back up the shingle and got the bus home to Ravendene. The bus smelt like a dinosaur had squeezed its way in and then pissed for the first time in years. It was a far cry from my glory days with Kimmy, tapping her mum's credit card and getting cabs everywhere!

When I got home there was no sign of my mum or my dead-beat brother, Jesus, aka JJ, just the gruesome two-some, my minging little sisters She-Ra and Evil-Lyn, whinging on about something; I shoved them out the way and barged straight into Mum's bedroom, where I knew she'd be, sitting on her bed surrounded by all our old baby clothes, bawling her eyes out. I perched on the side of the bed and looked at her sympathetically.

'It's not gonna happen, you know, Ma,' I said.

'Give it time,' she sniffed.

'You're, what are you, thirty-eight?'

'I'm thirty-five! I had you when I was eighteen. I thought it was best to wait – see a bit of life first.'

I laughed – hollowly, I hoped. The silly cow wasn't being funny, anyway she didn't mean to be. 'Whatever . . . don't you think you're clocking on a bit to have another brat?'

'I want to hold a tiny body in my arms just one more time,' she says.

'What d'you want a new brat for? What about those two freaks out there?'

'Oh, they're all grown up now—'

'– they're TEN! –'

'– AND they've got red hair. I've got you and Jesus, with your lovely black hair – I'd like to try for a little blonde, like me.'

'Then shag an albino!' I got up off the bed and slammed out. I don't know, it pissed me off to hear Susie talking about babies as if they were handbags – it got me thinking about Renata. My little Ren. Now resident somewhere out there in the wide blue yonder with her nonce of a father.

Everyone I loved had gone, fucked off, left me. Kim, Mark, Ren. And here I was, stuck in an out-of-season seaside town. As I said, things could only get better. Of course, I could've packed up and gone to London that very night. But think about it. A gorgeous chick like me, penniless, all alone in the big city – I'd be shooting up and kneeling down before you could say 'Pretty Woman With A Crack Habit'.

A job – that was what I had to get. Get a job, get some money together, get the hell out of Dodge – where I would forever be the bad guy/slaggy girl – and find Ren, or myself, or some easy mark I could live off. Go abroad maybe – I could see myself living the good life, chasing the sun. Sitting on a balcony somewhere, feet up, glass in hand, no worries. Sweet.

Funny how things change. A year ago I really thought I was happy. After my mad, bad time with Kim I'd had a MAJOR moment of weakness for tall, dark, delicious Mark and somehow we'd ended up married and with Ren to show for it. So there I was all tucked up cosy with hubby and daughter. Then one night me and him had a row about the average life expectancy of an Alsatian dog, and before I knew it I was down Lost Vegas getting off with this well-fit guy. A few alcopops later and we're doing it on the beach – then his mate turns up. Well, a girl needs time to prepare for these things, I always think. So I grabbed my empty bottle, halved it and stuck it in. Should of seen the blood. So I panicked, called Kizza, she comes running with her slaggy mum's credit card and before you can say 'Rug muncher' we're having a right old roll-around in this lush penthouse at the top of this posh London hotel. Sweet, it was. Morning after, coppers at the door, handcuffs on, bye-bye, Kim, hello clinker.

And you know, though I'm not advocating breaking a bottle in half and sticking it in some random guy forcing himself on you and being put in the clinker for the best part of year, it was certainly a bit of a wake-up call. It makes you decide whether you're gonna sink or swim – or even worse, tread water in the shallow end all your life. And what I wanted was to make a big splash. Or at least make a living. Or at least live – not just survive.

Well, the way I looked at it, I'd tried being wild – didn't work. Tried settling down – ditto. The thing I hadn't tried was being a sensible single girl – sorry, *woman* – making her way in the world. Sort of like *Sex and the City*, but without the sex. Or the city, really, no matter what Brighton calls itself. It's just a town – a town that's up itself, with good shops and clubs, but a town all the same.

So, not so much sex in the city as toil in the town, at least till the offer I couldn't refuse came along. But doing what? It's not like I was exactly overqualified. If only they gave out degrees in shoplifting or shooting pool, I'd be a Bachelor of Kiss-My-Ass! The job situation in Brighton isn't exactly a streets-paved-with-gold scenario either. Bastard seaside towns – either packed with tourists and not an inch on the beach or a drink in a club to be had without waiting an hour, or quiet as the grave and pissing down.

If you're not some up-yourself London gaylord with the world of computers at your fingertips, or else some yummy mummy with a tubby hubby who's got the flashy cashy, it can be pretty hard living down here, despite the candy-stripes and the carousels and the big blue to console you. 'London prices, Brighton wages,' goes the old saying – tell me about it! Basically, at my end of the barrel – which is the bottom, let's not mess about – you can either do seasonal work – on the pier or in the souvenir shops – or you can do domestic stuff – brats, cleaning, cleaning brats – or you can wait on some fat-arsed snobs in restaurants; not even bars at my age, which might've been OK, considering all the buckshee booze you'd get to pour down your neck. Or perhaps – oh, joy! – I could bury my youth and beauty in a call centre. Jeez, talk about spoilt for choice!

And of course they all pay shit wages. It's messed up, this. You think of a job that's cushy or enjoyable – actor, singer, model, whatever – and they all pay like a fortune. But you think of a job that's really demanding, or crap, and they pay peanuts. What's that all about! Should be the other way round by rights. No wonder girls go on the game.

So it was with a heavy heart that I trudged down to the jobcentre next day. Mind you, I say 'trudged', but it was more like 'sashayed'. 'Shimmied', even! One thing I've learned in this life so far: the less you've got the more front you've got to show – it's all very well for posh girls to grab a crumpled old shawl and just dab a touch of blusher on their mugs and flit out the door without even brushing their hair, but I don't feel dressed without a faceful of slap. And of course, That Walk; the Sugar Strut, like four stoned puppies fighting in slo-mo in a partitioned sack – two in front, two behind! It's hard for me to tone down my walk – it's my trademark – but I didn't want to overdo the glam-our and piss off the pen-pushers at the jobcentre. So I settled for pale pink pedal pushers, a shocking-pink bomber jacket and puce wedges. Only two earrings – two in each ear, that is – two shades of eyeshadow and one coat of Marvelash. And for the rest I went 'au naturel', as they say – nude lipgloss rather than lipstick, cheek stain rather than blusher and crimped hair instead of proper straight-ened. I must've looked like one of those demented milkmaid bints you see pictures of, prancing around with buckets on a stick across their shoulders, I was that undone-up.

Didn't do no use though – I knew this old dyke didn't

like me the minute I set eyes on her. Shame, 'cos I could have done with a bit of a hand up from the Muffia. So I start outlining the sort of thing I see myself being suited to – actress, model, whatever you call those sluts who go around dressed like cowboys shooting tequila out of guns. Then SHE comes back with all this stuff I'm SO not feeling: waitress, cleaner, CALL CENTRE! Like, NOT!

'Look,' I said quietly. I figured it was time to play my trump card. 'I might look like a flashy, gorgeous piece of aye-uss –' I always pronounce it like that, American-like – 'but I'm, YOU KNOW, one of your lot.'

The old bird looked at me blankly.

'A rug muncher,' I said helpfully, a bit louder this time. 'I've got my LIQUOR LICENCE! Geddit? I'M A DYKE, LIKE YOU!'

You know, Kizza always said I didn't know how loud I was, and I guess the little know-all was right on this one occasion. Whatever, the room had fallen silent and everyone was looking.

'Miss Sweet,' she says, all uptight like, 'I am a mother of three children and grandmother to four. I am not, and have never been, as you so delicately put it, a dyke. Let alone the other things.'

The silence had stopped now, that was the good news – but the sniggering had started, that was the bad. So that being the case, I thought I might as well be hung for a sheep as a creep, and went for the big laugh.

'Well, lady, if that's the case, why are you wearing prison shoes and a moustache I could hang my thong on?'

She looked at me dead nasty for a moment – and then she smiled. And I knew that smile weren't sweet, not one bit. She reached into her little box of tricks and handed me a pink bit of paper. And that's how I started my tour of Hell.

2

As I slogged up Clifton Hill in the pissing rain I knew I was in for a crap time. I've got this thing about going up hills – too much like hard work, like having phone sex. Trust me, nothing good ever waits at the top of them – not even Clifton, with its lush white houses and swank blue plaques. So I was expecting something bad. But not QUITE as bad as Baggy and Aggy.

Of course, I didn't recognize their names on the paper. 'Messrs Agnew & Bagshawe require a household help, live out. Must be a size 10, to double as pattern model.'

But we'd all read in the *Argus* about the pair of loaded old rag-trade queens who'd decamped down from London a while back and were tucked up well tidy in their big house, polishing their gewgaws and wearing out their jimjams. The minute I got inside the place I recognized it from a photo spread in *Hello!* – all dark and plush and hello sailor. For a minute I thought I'd fallen on my feet – I mean, household help no, but model YESSS! And they were gaylords, so no wandering mitts, obvo.

Then I clocked the mush on old Baggy – or was it Aggy. About as tall as an oversized toast soldier, head appropriately like a boiled egg with a face drawn on, mouth like a little cat's butt, looking at me like something the cat had pissed on, then dragged in. A real casing-the-joint look, from my head to my toes and back again – and he wasn't interested in the bod, I can tell you. I just KNEW that he was pricing every last thing I was wearing to the nearest 50p. And let's face it, most of it didn't cost much more than 50p.

'I've come about the job,' I said helpfully. 'The modelling and that—'

'The – OH, the CLEANING,' he snickered. 'Well . . . you're hardly a size ten, are you, dear?' He looked at my tits, and I swear he was the first man in my life to look at them with something like disgust. Though it could have been envy, the old tart. 'Not with that pair of cantaloupes!'

'That's funny – most people compare them to melons!'

'Are you for real . . . my word, you are, aren't you? The perfect real, synthetic thing.' He stood back and looked me up and down again, not so nastily this time. 'You've got nice small hips, I'll give you that. Not so much childbearing as Caesarean-demanding.'

'Size ten hips, size sixteen tits. Good, innit!'

'Hmm . . . the hips of a boy, the tits of a blow-up toy . . . I think I'm starting to . . . FEEL something . . .'

'So long as it's not my tits!' I leered.

The little cat's butthole in the middle of his face grew even tighter. 'Hardly, dear. AGGY!' he yelled. 'Get your worthless BTM down here and have a look at what the cat dragged in for us to play with!'

Then Aggy walks in – rolls in, rather. Boy, what a pair – one's bald as a coot, the other's fat as a pig. And, believe it, these people make a well lush living telling women how they should look! So Aggy treats himself to a good eyeful too, and immediately I can tell that though Baggy might diss him in front of strange – very strange! – girls, Aggy's the boss. That's cos he's the brains – though that don't make Baggy the beauty, no way! See, whereas old Baggy was just sort of toying with me when he sized me up, it's like Aggy is calculating my worth, and not just that of my clothes, down to the nearest 50p. More, what I'm worth to HIM.

'Turn around, dear.' I did as I was told, surely a first for me. 'Well, there's certainly quite a lot going on there, isn't there? "Everybody works!" as they used to say in vaudeville.'

'In what-ville?'

'Never mind – before your time.' He narrowed his eyes at me, all calculating like. 'Hmm – so you came about the cleaning job, did you?'

'Well – that and the modelling—'

'Love-bucket, I specified a size ten to cut my patterns on. Not a full-on Miss Tits to hire out by the hour.' He sighed. 'Still, they say that burlesque is back. And no one could deny that you could easily pass for a hoochy-coochy dancer from a Tijuana pony show.' He turned to Baggy. 'Well, I suppose I can stand to look at her if you can. At least she doesn't smell. Hire her!'

Tragically, I was well pleased; hey, they may have been freaks, but they were freaks with a good address and, let's face it, I'd had precious little of that. Remember, I grew up on the thirteenth floor – unlucky for some! – of ASBO Towers, give or take the odd stay at Her Maj's Pleasure, if not mine. The big white houses on the seafront, in the squares and up Clifton Hill – up which I now trudged again in the pissing rain on my first day working for Baggy and Aggy – were so foreign to ordinary Brighton kids that they might as well have been made of icing sugar and located on the moon. The only time kids from the Ravendene Estate saw the inside of a Regency house was when they were robbing it!

'What's the point in going on holiday if you live in a holiday town?' my mum used to say every summer when I'd moan at her about taking us abroad. That time me and Kizza legged it was the first time I'd ever stayed in a hotel even!

So despite the rain and the hill, I was well happy to be on my way to somewhere clean and quiet, and trying to keep a lid on my excitement at what lay in store for me. You could say I was in a holiday mood even! And as their lush house came into view, I even started dreaming that maybe, just maybe, if things went well and we got along, I might even become their – what's the word – muse, yeah, their 'muse', and they might ask me to move in with them. Peace and quiet and cleanliness – and, more importantly, a well central shag palace where I could drag fit French-language students back to instead of doing it on the beach, because Ravendene was way far out and they always lived in manky lodgings with some uptight landlady.

Quiet . . . I've always been a loud cow, but the older I got – all of seventeen – the more the non-stop racket at mine got totally on my tits. It had been even worse since my minging twin sisters had formed a rap group called 'Swearers Three', of all the dumb-ass things, with the little girl from the corner shop, Rajinder. Before school in the morning, after school in the afternoon, on weekend nights when Raj slept over, I had heard their cretinous intro/theme song so often that I was actually hearing it in my dreams, even when they too were asleep.

> 'Swearers One! – let's have some fun!
> Swearers Two! – I'll swear with you!
> Swearers Three! – come swear with me!
> One – two – THREE!'

Followed by a right mouthful, of course. I ask you, how much practising does that take. 'Sides, Ravendene kids are cursing before they can walk – rehearsing shouldn't come into it, they're naturals.

So with this ringing in my ears 24/7, can you really blame me for my uncharacteristically naive dreams as I rang the Baggy-Aggy bell that day? Well, I had just finally got clean from my drug habit, and therefore wasn't in my right mind. I saw myself being sat down for elevenses that very morning, my dainty feather-duster being gently extracted from my delicate fingers by Baggy as Aggy poured me a double gin from a piss-elegant Regency porcelain teapot and told me that to make an exquisite creature like myself sweat and strain over squalid domestic drudgery was quite like . . . I dunno, sticking a peacock down an S-bend.

Making Bambi live in a bucket. You know – just WRONG. And that all I needed to do to earn my daily pay – say, fifteen pound an hour, because it was like CREATIVE now – was just stand there staring into space, all enigmatic like, while they draped lush material on me and consulted each other in low, awed voices. Sweet . . .

I was still queening it over my tragic kingdom when the door lurched open and Baggy was standing there shooting evils up at me. 'The courtesy of kings?' he spat, barring my way with his dinky foot.

'The . . . queen of . . . clubs?' I answered weakly, thinking it was some sort of gay game.

'No, Marie!'

'Maria,' I pointed out reasonably. 'Ave-Maria Sweet, on the dotted line, but you can call me Sugar.'

'Really? Well, TARDY is what I call you.'

'Steady on!' I protested. He didn't know nothing about my sex life!

'Yes, tardy! That means LATE, in case you're not familiar with the word!' He held out his wrist to me, showing me a crap Barbie watch that even the Teat Twins would have chucked in the bin. 'What time do you call THIS!'

I peered at it. 'Um . . . three minutes past nine?'

'EXACTLY! And those three minutes are minutes I will never, ever be able to get back again. And THAT, Marie, is why punctuality is the courtesy of kings! Because to a CREATIVE person, every minute is a monarch! A monarch which you have seen fit to behead, three times over, with the casual weapon of your tardiness!' I must've looked the way I felt, totally amazed and confused, because he then threw in, '*Comprendez?*'

Oh, I GOT that. '"Understand" – right?'

You'd have thought I'd accused him of intercourse, the way he reacted – drew himself up to his full four foot nothing and stamped his stunted flipper like a crazy thing. 'YES! – UNDERSTAND!' He grabbed me by my arm but it wasn't in a loving caring way like I'd planned, taking the duster from my hand and making me the official Baggy-Aggy muse. Instead, with a brute force worthy of any Ravendene wife-beating bully, he seized my wrist and dragged me into the house, slamming the door behind me. 'Understand, Marie, that you are here to facilitate OUR creation! And that we are NOT here to facilitate your recreation, or your PROCREATION, or any of the other AYSHUNS that YOUR PEOPLE use as an excuse to waste OTHER PEOPLE'S time and spoil OTHER PEOPLE'S lives!'

You could have knocked me down with a Fetherlite; what did THREE FUCKING MINUTES matter in the grand scheme of things, or even in the skanky schedule of a couple of woofters? 'Hang about, mate – chill out—'

'I AM "chilled", "mate"!' Baggy hissed. 'I am so chilled, you could shake a perfect Martini in my skull!' He held out one of those dirty great checked plastic laundry bags – and somehow I just knew it wasn't packed with sumptuous swatches of velvets and satins, and rough-cut patterns just itching to be fitted on my nubile young body, and accessories which I'd be allowed to take home if I really,

REALLY liked at the end of long day's musing. Nope – because they didn't smell of ammonia, disinfectant and beeswax, to my knowledge. 'And this, love-bucket – this is all yours. Why don't you give it a twirl? And when you've got every surface in the place so shiny that you can see your pretty face in it, then YOU can chill too. It should only take, ooh, six hours! Ciao!'

And with that the front door slammed and I was alone in my tragic kingdom, with my mop sceptre and scrunchy crown. So of course I did what anyone would have done faced with such indignity – I sat down on the sofa, turned on the telly, found *Trisha* and lit up a spliff. Worker's play-time!

3

'One day I was walking to Asda, just chillin' in the sun
When suddenly it struck me, swearing big-time would be
*   fun!*
In the underpass, I shouted, "Ass!" and who should I see
But a slick little chick giving it a go, shouting, "Ho!" right
*   back at me!*

Then a third girl, called Rajinder, from the Paki shop—'

I'd had enough. It was only eight in the morning, Saturday, and being woken up by the little bastards after two weeks of toil and torment at the hands of Aggy and Baggy was bad enough, but now they were being racist too – well, Kimmy had told me how bad that was, judging by appearances, and I could see it now, the vile ginger twats. I dragged myself out of my pit, opened my bedroom door and opened my gat-trap to give them a right bosting.

'SHUT THE SWINE UP, YOU EVIL LITTLE—'

I found the big brown eyes of little Raj, bless, looking up at me. 'Sorry, Ria. Did I wake you up?'

I pulled my Topshop negligee tight around me. 'It's not you, sweetheart. It's those effing brat sisters of mine. Singing a song like that – and making you sing it too!' I looked around. 'Where are they?'

'They're at a Brownie boot sale for the elderly. Your

mum said it was OK if I came round here and practised cos my dad don't know I'm in Swearers Three. MY song, innit!' she smirked.

Frankly, I was scandalized. 'Oh really, mademoiselle! Your parents – I don't know 'em, but I know the type, because I bullied their younger brothers and sisters at school, regretfully – are gonna be SO PLEASED that you're boasting about being a swearer. And a Paki – and the word is Pakistani, by the way!'

She had the grace to look ashamed. 'Actually we're Punjabi. But if I said "Punji shop", no one would know what I mean.'

'Well, whatever. I need to get my beauty sleep, so keep it down.' Then something occurred to me. 'Here. Your parents don't want any help at the Paki – sorry, Punji – shop, do they?'

'Not from round here,' she said straight back, the cheeky little mare. 'My mum says, "Raver behind the till, your profits get ill." Good, innit! She's going to write a song for Swearers Three too, but without the swearing.'

'I'll be listening out for it on the radio,' I said sarkily. 'Well, good luck, but practise somewhere else, OK? I've had a pig of a week and I need a good zizz.'

'Right, Ria,' she whispered, putting her finger to her lips and tiptoeing off. I couldn't help smiling – she was a lovely little thing. Shame she couldn't have been my sister instead of the ginger mingers; if Susie REALLY wanted to have another baby, I wondered if I could get her to do it with a Punjabi guy.

I staggered back to bed, groaning. When I'd settled on to the Baggy-Aggy chaise longue that first day, spliff in hand, I never dreamed how hard my working week was going to turn out to be. I only watched *Trisha* and had a little nap, and when I woke up it was the afternoon and there was a message on the phone from Baggy saying they'd be back at three – I darted round that place with a broom up my arse, literally, before finding a second message saying that they'd be back at eight instead! And by the smile in Baggy's voice, I knew he'd planned it that way.

And then I came in at nine sharp the next morning, and the house which I'd left looking like something gone over by Kim and Aggie now looked like something done over by the inmates of Battersea Dogs Home. And it had been that way ever since; leave it immaculate three nights a week, find it a tip next time. By the second Friday night, I felt like I had housemaid's knee, athlete's foot and, for all I knew, water on the brain. I felt like zero. And I was just £110.60 the richer a week. Before tax.

I lay there in bed, thinking about my alleged 'job'. What a tragic farce! My mum used to have a friend, Natalia, who was a cleaner for this woman in Hove – you wouldn't believe the perks! Ten quid an hour basic, two weeks in the Canaries every year and a few little extras that weren't exactly legal. This broad was always creeping up on Nat and unplugging the vacuum cleaner and making her go out on the piss with her because she was 'blocked', whatever that is, and 'seeking inspiration' – she was a writer or something. Natalia told my mum they were like sisters, but in the end they fell out over a packet of wine gums, of all the weird things.

As I lay there in my bed of pain, my scullery-maid's elbow give me gyp, I reflected sourly that I'd be lucky to get even a lick of an empty wine gum wrapper from B&A. I'd taken a Jammie Dodger from their 'retro-trash' cupboard on my second day there – and found the cost of the entire packet subtracted from my wages. This, from a pair of ponces that spent fifty pounds a day on flowers from Florian the Florist!

Get this. Yesterday, while having a bit of a poke about – sorry, 'a thorough clean' – I found all these leather albums at the bottom of one of them long things that looks like a sort of padded bench but isn't – the seat opens up, like a box. Inside there was loads of sheets and linen, dead innocent, but I had this sort of instinct that there was something worth seeing underneath it all.

Well, there were half a dozen of these big red books at the bottom of the bed stuff, and soon as I opened up the first one I realized it was Baggy and Aggy's scrapbooks, bless 'em! You could see why they kept 'em hidden – a) because they photographed like such a pair of freaks and b) because, well, it hardly fitted their image, did it, to be saving their old yellow clippings like a pair of soft schoolgirls! Not with them so cool and cutting edge and techno; the idea of them sitting down with scissors and paste – Aggy constantly criticizing Baggy's cutting and pasting techniques! – made me feel all warm and gurgly inside, a bit like foreplay. Well, by that time I could have done with a good laugh, so I turned on *Jeremy Kyle*, sat down with a bottle of Sunny V – Sunny D with a splash of vodka – and I treated myself.

It weirded me out at first, seeing them posing and poncing around the very house – the very room! – I was now slurping my Sunny V in: haughty in *Hello!*, impish in *Interiors*, wussy in *Wallpaper*. I skimmed through the interviews and couldn't help laughing; in every single one, there was some reference to how much they loved women, respected women, worshipped women, designed their clothes to make women feel good. Oh, come ON! Yeah, *right*. I'd heard Baggy on the phone once to one of his mucky-minded mockers: 'Yep, the minute I popped out of my dear mama, I knew right away that I never wanted to go back into one of those hellholes again,' he'd sniggered. Of course, doing his bum-chum up the wrong 'un must be *so* much more hygienic!

And it struck me as I read this drivel that you can say what you like about lezzies – bad shoes, rubbish tits, scary voices; only kidding! – but you have to hand it to them, they don't do this bogus gay man equivalent of going around telling the world how much they love, respect and worship men while doing everything in their power to avoid having any contact more intimate than an air kiss with them. And this made me think of Kizza, and all the sweet times we'd had, and before I knew it I was lying face down on the floor crying like a baby.

Which is probably why I didn't hear Baggy and Aggy come in.

Well, I thought fast and said that I'd found the albums

while I was 'doing a linen inventory' and that I couldn't resist looking at them because I was 'such a fan'. Believe me, a man's a man, gay or straight, and nothing wipes their memories or soothes their tempers faster than a bit of flattery. Baggy gets sent to the kitchen to make me what Aggy calls a *'tasse de Twinings'* – a mouldy old cup of tea to you and me – and Ag himself actually goes so far as to sit his fat ass down with me on the sofa and pat me rather cautiously on the back!

'Now, love-bucket,' he goes, 'what's all THIS about?'

'All what?' I snivel, reluctant to admit some sucker has actually caught me crying.

He gives this little shudder of disgust, which let me tell you is REALLY comforting. 'The red eyes, the streaming nose, the puffy face – uck!' Cheers, mate! But I felt a bit better when he went on, 'Pretty girls should never cry, they ruin themselves. Every pretty girl should have a plain girl to do all her crying for her. Like a whipping boy.'

'Saucy!' I said, nudging him. It's amazing how any sort of flattery cheers me up – uh-oh, so it's not just men then! – even from a snobby old woofter.

'Easy, tiger lily!' he winced. Baggy was sort of hovering in the doorway, and Aggy clicked his fingers at him. 'Begone, Bag-features! – I must seek the soul of our pikey princess!'

Well, I didn't much like the sound of that, but it turned out to be well sweet. Like my sixth shoplifting sense, I sort of knew what he wanted to hear. And so I told him about Kimmy, and her being in love with me, and me being in love with her when it was too late. And his eyes got bigger and bigger, and his face got closer and closer and then his arms opened up and he grabbed me and held me and cried, 'My poor baby! So you're NOT a breeder after all! What a horrid time you've had – we must do something lovely for you . . .'

And then he'd pulled away, and I'd pulled myself together and gone home. And so here I was, two weeks into my career as a cleaner to the Brighton flitterati, wondering if anything new truly lurked around the corner, or whether it was just a load of camp cobblers. Whatever, I wouldn't know until Monday morning, so I might as well get my kip while I could.

I felt myself finally drifting off into sleep . . .

'Then a third girl, called Rajinder, from the Paki shop,
Joined our cussing crew, and the dissing didn't stop!
The lesson art, when swearing starts, colour doesn't count –
Black, white, brown or yellow, come and curse in large
amounts!'

4

Well, do me three different ways if on Monday morning B&A didn't have a nice surprise for me. I let myself in and there in the kitchen, instead of a can of Cif, a used-up old Brillo pad and a note telling me to keep my mitts off their Party Rings, there were the boy-toyers themselves with scissors, tape measures and rough paper laid out on the table in front of them.

Baggy gave me a sickly grin, like Santa the morning after a night down the the K-hole. 'Surprise!'

Aggy stood up and waddled towards me, taking my hand. 'Sit down, my dear.' Well, my philosophy is never stand when you can sit and never sit when you can lie, so I was well up for this unexpected development. But what came next really floored me.

'Maria, we feel we have misjudged you,' he said solemnly. I put on this marge-wouldn't-melt expression, all the time wondering furiously what the snooty swines had been judging me as – and the CHEEK that this pair of freaks had been judging anybody fair rendered me speechless too, which was lucky. 'Until last Friday, we thought you were – well, I won't mince words –' About the only thing you wouldn't mince, mate! – 'we thought you were a typical chavette. An under-educated, over-made-up breeder, to be blunt. Just one of those Ravendene drones that's pregnant at fifteen, a grandma by thirty and quite frankly fit only for cat meat by forty –' He shuddered, then brightened up. 'But you're not – you're a baby dyke! You're one of us!'

Well, this was what you called a backhanded compliment and being damned with faint praise rolled into one, I figured as I smiled sweetly back at Aggy. On one hand it was a change not to be written off as a pikey pillock for once – but on the other hand, did I really want to join Aggy and Baggy's gang? I mean, look at the pair of 'em! – walking wounded when it came to looks, for sure. Came off the wrong end of a scrap with the ugly stick, and then some. I've noticed this quite a lot during my short life, as a matter of fact – that those who put others down for being ugly, thick, having no style and all that are often complete mingers themselves; it's like they've got a magic mirror stashed somewhere telling them they're the fairest of them all, whereas in reality they haven't got a – short, fat, hairy – leg to stand on. 'Cept me, natch – I insult mingers from the solid ground of supreme beauty!

But the main thing that really made me swear behind my smile and want to bite the hand that was now trying to force-feed me compliments was that he was more or less describing my mum with that nasty little number about Ravendene breeders. OK, so Susie had had me at eighteen rather than fifteen – she'd wanted to see a bit of life first, remember! – but I could see her daft sweet smiling face as clearly as if she was standing in front of me when Aggy shuddered at the idea of breeders. And then course there was me and Ren – unknown to them their little dyke was also a dirty horrid breeder after all. And you know, there's lots of good things about gayers – they always know where to get good E, and their club nights are banging – but there is this horrible way a lot of them, down here in Brighton at least, seem to see straight people, particularly working-class women, as these dumb cows just chewing cud and churning out kids whose hungry little mouths are eating up their disposable income that might better be spent on handjobs and man-bags. They're always writing narky letters to the papers complaining that their taxes have to pay for schools and that – but if the breeders didn't breed where would the hairdressers come from that save their lives when they've given themselves a bad fringe while off their nuts on Special K? Be real, they couldn't clone 'em off a big old gay conveyor belt – they want to thank the breeders for breeding their servants for them! No, the way I look at it, we're all in it together; it's not meant to be like the War-locks and the e-boys or whatever in that mental film about the time machine that Samantha Mumba was in.

But I didn't say none of this – just grinned and nodded like a loved-up toy doggy in the back window of some sad car.

'And so,' Aggy continued, 'we've been thinking that we might proffer ourselves as guardian angels, of a kind. Men-tors, without the mauling which usually characterizes raw young girl/sophisticated gent relationships. Patrons, with-out the poking—'

'Sugar daddies without the wandering hands,' butted in Baggy eagerly.

'Oh, that's well weird! Everybody calls me Sugar anyway!'

Aggy closed his eyes. 'Then the matter seems to be settled. Mmm . . . sugar, sweet, decay, rot . . . the immediate gratification and inevitable comedown of modern life, the eternal limbo of the morning after . . .' His eyes snapped open. 'Well, what are you waiting for? Strip!'

Why is it that I bring out the beast in the most unlikely people? Even Kim Lewis, the last virgin in captivity. And now Baggy and Aggy were set on grooming me for a right old menagerie – even gaylords wanted a bit of Sugar-shoving! I was sick of it frankly. I stood up.

'Thanks for the offer, Mr Agnew. But I'm gay, as I've just explained to you. And I really don't think I can change my sexuality on demand like that, just so you and Mr Bagshawe can get a bit of girl-booty for a change.'

I realized I'd made a mistake when B&A's eyes grew huge with amazement and then disgust. I was edging towards the door, aiming to cut and run, when they erupted in twin explosions of laughter. They doubled up, they held on to each other, they pointed at me with shaky fingers while wiping tears from their eyes. I stopped in my tracks and stared at them.

'What's so funny?'

'Oh, Maria . . .' gasped Baggy, 'the idea that we'd ever want to . . . HAVE SEX . . . with . . . with YOU, of all people!' And their hilarity resumed.

'Thanks a lot!' I snorted. I'm not used to getting a kickback, even from benders. Many's the time I've scored with a buff batty in the Ladies' at Revenge when it's chucking out time and he don't want to go home empty-handed.

Aggy pulled himself together, breaking away from Baggy and coming up to me. 'Maria, sweet. Sweet Maria. It's nothing personal. It's not that we don't like you – it's just that we don't like what you've got going on in your thong. But everything else about you we love, from the top of your fierce scrunchied head to the tip of your dance-calloused toes. Even your name – Maria Sweet! – well, say it loud and there's music playing. In short, everything about you screams 'Muse!'. And it's something we can use.' He took my face in his hands. '"To double as a pattern model" – you saw the card. Except you won't just be some random arrangement of flesh we use as target practice before we show our clothes on some stuck-up coked-out size-six super.' He tucked a strand of hair behind my ear ever so tenderly. 'You'll be our top girl. Our first lady. What do you say, Sugar?'

I blinked. And the blink of an eye was all it took for me to make up my mind. I wrenched myself out of his grasp and stared at him, sneering like Elvis in a Wonder-bra. I pulled open my shirt, buttons flying amok.

'Do you want me just topless, or everything off?'

Aggy gaped, then grinned. 'You can leave your thong on. Lest we run screaming in terror. But everything else should come off.'

Everything else came off in a flash. And the weirdest

thing was, naked in front of them I felt for the first time invulnerable. As though I was wearing armour, even.

When I let myself into Sweet Towers that night, I was tingling all over; it was a bit like having pleasurable pins and needles, which was appropriate because I'd spent the day having paper patterns pinned on me, and watching Baggy and Aggy give each other the needle something rotten. You read a lot about 'the creative process' when fashion designers give interviews to the magazines, and now at last I'd had the chance to experience it at first hand, as Creatives put their hands all over me. And as far as I could tell, the creative process was a lot like PMT, but as if an opera singer was suffering from it – everything amped up to the max. Or in this case, two opera singers, who wanted to take each other's nuts off with pinking shears.

It was a right weird one to be a girl, standing there in all my naked glory, and have two gaylords fighting over me – especially two gaylords who'd previously believed I was only good for pumping out puppies and sponging off same-sex citizens! Yet suddenly I'd morphed from slapper to goddess and they were pulling each other's extensions out to get first go at my arse. In a purely artistic way, of course.

'NOOOO!' Aggy had yelled at Baggy, wrenching a tape measure from his hand and flinging it across the room. 'We're not making drip-dry crimplene frocks for the mother of the bride somewhere in Surrey, here! We're walking on the edge, wearing a blindfold, without a safety net!

So why are you trying to dress her like a woman called . . . I don't know, HILARY!'

'AGS! It was only three fingers beneath no-man's-land!'

'Three fingers be damned! Two fingers' modesty is all a girl needs before the cellulite kicks in. You take your three fingers, Bag-features, and stick them where the sun don't shine!'

'What, Manchester?!'

It goes on like this for six hours solid, and all the time they're bickering and bitching and swooning and crooning and groaning and grinning, but the point is, THEY'RE DOING IT BECAUSE OF ME! I'm no longer the skivvy that clears up after them, but the focus of the thing that matters to them most in the world – their creativity. OK, so it was a bit weird how suddenly I was the perfect model – I mean I might have been a dyke but I was still a gorgeously curvy one. Yet I've always had a funny effect on people, got their juices flowing, just that in Ags and Bags' case it was creative ones, not the sort you have to clean up after. Plus – only a total fruit-loop would look a job this cushy in the eye and start asking questions. By the time I emerged from Chez Bag-Ag, I was walking on air.

'Mum! MUM! SUUUZE!' I called as I slammed the door behind me. I had an extra fifty quid in my pocket 'for keeping so still and smelling so nice – for a girl!' as Baggy had charmingly put it, and I was going to take her straight down to Pizza Express in the Lanes for a proper meal out. Gnocchi, dough-balls, tonno e fagioli on the side – the works! Even a Ravello Bombe and half a bottle of house white so long as she didn't annoy me too much. No more Domino's for us, now I was a model – it was gonna be Sloppy Giuseppes all the way, and I don't just mean the drooling waiters. Who knows, I might even get a doggy bag for the gruesome twosome to scrap over!

I looked for Susie in the kitchen and the sitting room and when I couldn't find her I headed for the bedroom, thinking she'd be up to her old praying-for-a-baby tricks. I walked right in – and stone me if she wasn't sobbing her heart out, swigging from a bottle of gin, for all the world like a sailor about to be sent for a month in the Priory!

I crouched down beside her. 'Whassup, Suze?' She kept on sobbing, louder now. 'Mum?'

She looked up at me, her big blue eyes all red-rimmed in a dead white face. Sort of like a Union Jack somebody had done in a too-hot wash and it had come out a right runny old mess. 'Oh, Ave!'

I knew it was bad then; she only calls me Ave, as in Ave-Maria, when things are well dire. 'Come on, Suze – spit it out!'

'I wish I had!' She did that hard, mirthless laugh that I was so good at, but which I heard so rarely from her. 'Oh, Ave – I'm PREGNANT!'

'But I thought you—'

'I MADE A MISTAKE! I DON'T WANT IT! I CAN BARELY GET BY AS IT IS!' And she started up with the sobbing again.

It's a funny thing – I always thought I was quite cold. I've never gone in for a lot of hugging and kissing – 'cept with men, when they're fit, and I'm pissed, heh heh! In fact, I remember making Susie cry when I was only ten by exclaiming one night, 'Leave me alone, you lezzer!' when she tried to give me her usual kiss goodnight – I guess I was pretty scary even as a ten-year-old, because she never tried that move again. Ironic, really, in the light of what happened with old Kizza Lewis!

But now it was instinctive, like a lioness with its cub – the fierce protection I felt towards her. Poor old Suze, always picking the manky old Montélimar in the chocolate box of life. I took her dumb, precious body in my arms and noticed that she smelt of defeat.

And I whispered in her ear. 'Don't worry, Mum – I'll fix it.'

5

And this is a thing I've noticed about life – no sooner has Lady Luck laid down her cape to see you across that puddle of mud than Lord Muck swings by in his ride and splashes it all over you. That is, just when you're riding high is when something happens to bring you down. Happened with me and Kim, happened with me and Mark and Ren. And now here I was, taking my first faltering steps as a model, and I'd walked slap bang into some sort of freaking Channel 5 soap opera, with a pregnant mum I'd promised to fix up an abortion for!

'And not an NHS abortion, mind!' Susie added over a Domino's Dominator that night – somehow the idea of Pizza Express had lost its gloss. 'They treat you like a right slag, Natalia says.'

'So –' I pushed my box away, pizza only half eaten. 'What's the story? All that hoping and moping and banging on about wanting to hold a little body in your empty old arms again – what made you change your mind?'

'I just suddenly realized I was being irresponsible,' she said humbly. 'And that I didn't want to . . . waste my life – bringing up kids any more . . .'

This didn't sound one bit like Susie, and I looked at her suspiciously. 'That's something I thought I'd never hear you say – you sure?'

She pushed her pizza away too. 'Well – I didn't want

to say this, in case it made you feel bad. But I realized that all the time I thought I wanted another baby to be a mum to, I was kidding myself. What I really want, Ave, is to be a grandma. To little Ren.' She caught hold of my hand. 'I want you to find Ren, Ave. And bring her home.'

My times! – it was like being with Baggy and Aggy all over again. Find this, clear up that! 'You don't want much, Mum, do you!'

'We could hire a private detective—'

'With what? Fresh air?'

'I can do extra shifts—'

'Oh right – we'll get one from Toon-Town, and we'll pay them with the tiddlywinks that you call wages! Private abortions, private detectives – why don't you just pawn your silver spoon and use the cash from that!'

She looked right downcast at that, and I knew then that there was no way out of it – I'd have to use my modelling money, the money I'd been going to save to get the hell out of Dodge. 'OK – don't worry. I'll see to it.' I squeezed her hand and stood up. As I got to the door I turned. 'Here – you sure you don't just want to let me push you down the stairs and save us a wedge? Only joking!' I protested as her face got ready to crumple.

I went to bed with a heavy heart, though that could have been the Dominator. Whatever, it was like I was carrying a big weight in a moneybelt round my stomach. It was called responsibility, it was called being a grown-up – whatever, it sucked. I wished I could go down the beach and get blind on cheap vodka and pick up some random bloke and stab him after sex, like in the old, innocent days of my girlhood – but heck, I had a baby to abort and a baby to find.

I went to sleep and dreamed I had a baby who came out looking like the fifteen-year-old Kim Lewis, who then turned into a pizza with double pepperoni, which I gorged right down without it touching the sides. When I woke up, I was sick. I exited the bathroom to find Susie throwing up in the kitchen sink and the twins hurling on to the kitchen floor, obviously having raided the abandoned pizza boxes during the night. I fled the sickly scene as though the store detectives from hell itself were on my trail, desperate to return to the perfumed pincers of Baggy and Aggy.

'Pew-eee! – someone's had sausage for breakfast!' Bags complained as he leaned close to my face to pin a rough snood around my hair.

'Yes, and someone else *hasn't*,' Ags rebuked him. He was definitely the boss of the outfit, and though he wasn't averse to insulting me himself, he didn't like Baggy to overstep the mark. 'You feeling up to it, sugar-shovel? You can always go home if you're a bit punk.'

'I'm fine,' I assured him – the last thing I needed to lift my spirits was a return to the House of Barf. He was on his knees in front of me pinning a hem up on the shortest skirt imaginable, but with knickers attached. 'So what's the idea behind this one then?'

'Um – *White Boots*. Ever read that?'

'No. But it sounds well pervy.'

'Skating-starlet look – ice queen! It will be made of the finest red velvet, with matching muff!'

Baggy and I sniggered as one and Aggy gave us A Look; we giggled like kids and he tutted good-naturedly. It struck me then that I was really starting to value my time with them. And if that was so, maybe they were right about where I came from – not snobs, just knowledgeable. Maybe I'd been the one who was ignorant, not them. If they could have seen the vomit-fest I'd left that morning . . . I shuddered.

'You cold, pet?' Baggy asked through a mouthful of pins. 'Because we're going to have to take your skating suit off soon and try your princess number on. And goodness knows, that one fits where it touches. The finest black silk. Very minimalist. Very Audrey H.'

'No, I'm fine,' I said, holding my head up high. A princess, eh? If that's what they thought of me, that's what I could be. And if that's what they thought of me, I could trust them. 'Listen . . . I wasn't going to say anything, but I've got to get my mum an abortion. A proper one, in a private clinic – she's too scared to take that pill that brings it on, she wants to be unconscious, and she's heard nasty stuff about NHS ones. Can you advance me my wages?'

There was a silence, and then Aggy said, in a voice so soft and sincere it made me want to cry, 'Of course we can give you the money. But not as an advance – as a "quid pro quo". Do you know what that means, Maria?'

I thought about it logically. 'Is it something to do with money?'

'Even better than that, my sweet. It's something to do with friendship. And inspiration. And asking not what you can do for me, but what I can do for you . . .' He stood up, walked across the room, scrabbled in a man-bag, leaned on a table writing something and came back with a chéque. He handed it to me; I read it and almost wept.

I almost wept partly because of how big it was and how generous these people were, and how I'd misjudged them. But also because I didn't have a bank account and I was going to look like a right townie teat now. 'Um – any chance of cash, is there? Sorry to ask, but—'

'You don't have a bank account!' Baggy clapped his hands. 'Ooh, you get more perfect by the day, Tiny Tears!'

Aggy went back to his man-bag. 'Shut it, shim-face. Hmm, low on cash – Bags has been blowing it all on Immac and gin miniatures, no doubt.' He turned round and smiled at me. 'Sugar-shack, why don't you take a Red Bull break before we fit the Princess dress? Bags, you come out with me and we can pick up a crate of shampoo from Threshers while we're at it.'

I chuckled to myself as they left, Baggy grumbling that all Aggy needed him for was as 'a beast of burden, a donkey'! 'Shame you're not hung like one!' I heard Aggy snap before the door slammed.

I stepped out of my skating skirt and stood there in my leotard – it's sort of a body for snobs – stretching happily. I could get to like this model racket, I thought – just standing stock still with a couple of blokes down on their knees worshipping me. Felt . . . *natural*, somehow. And whereas when I first met them I thought they were this demonic double-act looking down their noses at me, now there were times when it definitely felt like me and Aggy having a laugh at Bags – like Ag'd recognized that I was, I dunno, a *superior* sort of person too, like him. I was starting to think that I'd been unfair on the both of them really.

I went towards the kitchen to grab a Red Bull when I felt the first stirrings of some bladder action. See, this is the difference between a professional model and an amateur – an amateur, left alone by her mentors, would use the break as an excuse to have a fag, pick at stuff from the fridge, maybe have a swig from something sticky on the drinks trolley and generally nose about, dead common. But being a proper model I decided I should answer the call of nature before I was pinned into my Princess dress. So I swerved and was heading for the downstairs toilet, as per, when a thought struck me.

I didn't WANT to use the downstairs dunny today. It seemed wrong, somehow. Look at me – conversing wittily with top fashion designers, about to be fitted for my Princess dress! I hadn't been into the en suite since I started modelling for them – some poor Croatian cow was cleaning up after them now – but my memories of it were well sweet. Apart from the huge marble bath, big enough to take my entire family – perish the thought, I'd drown them first! – there was the leopard-print toilet seat, the snow-leopard-print shag-pile carpet, the Bvlgari soaps, the shower that was also a tiny steam-room, the little telly on the adjustable stalk, the concealed stereo speakers, the mini fridge filled with Red Bull and champagne miniatures, the bog roll that was so soft and so white it seemed to have been made of flattened, stretched, perforated clouds – ooh, I'm not joking, I could have happily lived in there. There was nothing *wrong* with the downstairs lav, don't get me wrong – you could have eaten your tapas off it. It was just . . . ordinary. And ordinary was the last thing I felt . . .

I padded up the stairs in my scanties, feeling like a beautiful jewel thief . . . except I was the biggest jewel of all, heh heh! I figured that with a crate of champagne in mind, they'd be heading for the local Oddbins, where Aggy had a big crush on the surfer dude who worked there – there was bound to be a whole bunch of 'tasting' and 'sampling' going on, with Baggy reduced to gnashing his teeth in the background and then carting the box back up the hill, complaining bitterly that they could have caught a cab, while Aggy hissed that the workout would be good for him. I had half an hour, easy.

I walked into their bedroom, where I'd spent so many happy hours dossing on the king-size and going through the drawers when I was their servant rather than their muse. The shocking pink walls – 'Pomegranate' – and the gold leaf ceiling made it feel like a big old bling womb or something, and I almost purred with satisfaction that I'd made it so far, so quick – not only was there room at the top, but I was about to use the VIP lavvy!

I pushed open the en suite door – suite, Sweet! see, it was all falling into place – and I honestly couldn't have been more surprised if I'd discovered a unicorn having a bath with a dodo. Doing his thing at the privy was a naked, gorgeous, golden brown fifteen-year-old boy. And not just any naked, gorgeous, golden brown fifteen-year-old boy either – it was only Duane Trulocke, Jesus's best mate, used to hang at ours all the time when he needed to get away from his own excuse for a family. The last time I'd seen him, he'd been on the business end of my fist, when I caught him and Jesus perving over me as I was laying naked by my bedroom window on a whole roll of BacoFoil, trying to catch some rays on a cold but sunny winter day when I didn't have the readies for a spray-on!

'Duane! What you think you're playing at!'

He gasped and grabbed at a face flannel to cover his shame. Didn't really do much though, as he was a big boy for his age. 'Ria!'

'What you playing at, you little git! You robbing my mates?!'

He smirked. 'Do I look like I'm dressed for robbing?'

The smirk said more than the words. I felt well stupid. 'You might have . . . stripped off so you could squeeze through a narrow space—'

'Yeah, right!' He picked up a pair of boxers and pulled them on. 'That's probably why I'm greased too!' He laughed.

I just stood there gaping at him. Aggy, my mate . . . with an underage kid . . . and Baggy makes three! Annoying little twat that he was, Duane was almost family, in a pervy incestuous brother kinda way.

'Anyway, what you mean, your mates?' He took a flying

leap and landed on the bed. It looked really weird seeing dirty little Duane from the Ravendene Estate sitting there on all those rumpled Frette sheets – like some sort of porn video out the back of *Attitude*. 'Seeing how you're dressed, I'd say you was being paid for the same reason as me.' He sniggered. ''Cept you're a GIRL so they wouldn't have no use for you!'

'Get lost! I'm their model!'

'Yeah – *glamour. Full frontal!*'

I was just about to give him an encore of what he'd asked for that day on the BacoFoil, when I realized where I was. I couldn't go acting like some slapper down West Street on a Saturday night, I was a muse! And Duane, dirty little perve or not, was their . . . *lover* or something! And if I was going to be part of a more . . . I dunno, *civilized* set-up than what I was used to, I was going to have to act in a more civilized manner, I s'pose, and not react fist first, brain belatedly as I always had done.

So I folded my arms to keep my fists out of harm's way and left it at looking down my nose at him. 'I'm their muse, actually. I won't even ask if you know what that word means, but it's enough to say that what I do for Mr Agnew and Mr Bagshawe I do on my feet rather than on my knees.' With that I turned to go, but then something good and spiteful occurred to me, and I turned to smile over my shoulder. 'Talking of which, it wouldn't kill you to have a bit of a wash. Those sheets cost an arm and a leg – they don't want to have to send them to the cleaners every time you drop by for tea and *fairy cakes.*'

'Don't tell Jesus, right!! Please, Ria!' I heard his scared yelp as I closed the door. But not scared enough, apparently. As I started to go down the stairs, I heard a Ravendene upbringing triumph over fear, and a shameless cry of, 'NICE TITS!' These kids, they're dragged up, not brought up!

6

So a week later I was sitting in this waiting room of this private clinic, Susie having kittens – bad choice of cliché! – beside me. It might have been private, just like she wanted, but it was a right temple of gloom, I can tell you. They had some local Sussex pop radio station playing – fair play to them, they probably thought it would cheer the assembled tot-slayers up, but like, did it never occur to them that every other word in every other pop song is, like, 'baby'? 'My baby's gone . . . come back, baby . . . baby don't leave me . . .' It was like some mole from the pro-life side had got in under the wire and was doing their damned best to turn the poor broads at the eleventh hour. And they all sat there with faces like they just won a wet weekend in Wivelsfield, brooding on their imaginary babies. I mean, it's the wet indecisiveness I can't stand, in any part of life – do one thing or do the other, but for God's sake DON'T do one thing while wishing you could do the other! I've known that that's the quickest route to misery since I was six – a DOG probably knows it – an AMOEBA probably knows it! So why do adults have such a big problem working it out?

As if reading my thoughts, Susie said, with the suspicion of a sniffle, 'And the funny thing is, I've always been pro-life—'

'You still are,' I said briskly, trying to remember what

Kim had drummed into me about A Woman's Right To Choose; I felt a bit of a pang as I remembered how I'd always driven her mad by saying that I was more interested in A Woman's Right To Booze. 'Still,' I'd added cheekily, 'I s'pose they're the same thing really – I wouldn't want no one giving me evils for nine months every time I ordered an Aftershock!' Happy days . . . 'You're choosing a real life – yours – over a –' What was the word? Sounded like 'potato' – 'over a *putative* one.' On cue, some mad old singing bird started complaining that she couldn't find her baby, and Susie started sniffling again.

Me, though, I went off into a reverie, thinking about Kim . . . would I have to go all around the world to find her – or just to Pease Pottage? I had no idea where the Lewises had taken her. I must've been making a right mis old face, because Susie dragged herself away from her mope-fest and smiled bravely at me. 'I know what you're thinking about . . .'

What – Kim Lewis wearing nothing but a suntan, a scrunchy and a smile? 'I bet you don't!' I snorted.

'Yes I do. A mother always knows.' She patted my hand. 'You're thinking about how you'd search all round the world just to find your baby.'

'That's right!' I looked at her amazed. I didn't think she'd actually grasped it about me and Kim, that we were More Than Just Good Friends – 'But how can they, when they haven't got one!' was the one thing I recalled her saying about lesbians. And I wasn't about to draw her a diagram – I only did that in public, on walls, with an audience!

She patted my hand. 'Find her, love. Find Ren.'

'Yeah . . . course I will,' I muttered. Mental note: FIND REN. (And give her to Mum to look after while I go and find Kim.)

'She'll be walking . . . talking . . . they grow up in the flash of an eye.' Sniffles ahoy! 'Like this little one – soon it'll be moving—'

'Yeah, walking and talking and no doubt playing the violin, all before it's born!' I was getting exasperated now. 'Look, Mum, all this stuff you read in the papers about how bad abortion is – they've got an . . . invested agenda.' Trying to remember the gospel according to Kizza again! 'All they want women to do is stay at home and breed – that way there's less competition for the cushy jobs. Look, when the *Daily Mail* says, "Oh, it's moving about at three weeks!" or whatever, you want to take that with a pinch of salt – with a SHAKER of salt. I mean, motes of dust dance about in the air, and it's well cute and all that – but it doesn't mean they're ALIVE!'

'But I'm a Catholic!'

'So are the Italians, Mum – and they've got the lowest birth rate in Europe!' I was really quite glad now that I'd listened to Kim between our sex bouts, though it had seemed well boring at the time. 'And, um, one in four pregnancies ends in a miscarriage so, you know, you're just helping Mother Nature along really. And you're less likely to be depressed after an abortion than after a baby . . . and best of all you won't get any new stretch marks! Because face it, Mum, you already look like a zebra with your kit off!'

'I know you're right, love, I just—' Susie's putative words of wisdom were obscured by a burst of laughter from a group of staff ladies in the corner. I said it was a temple of gloom, but that was just the punters – the workers were well smiley. You'd have thought it was a cocktail party rather than a den of abortion!

I checked in my bag. There it was – five hundred pounds, cash. Sweet.

'But that's more than I need!' I'd squealed like a priss when Aggy'd handed the wad over shortly after my brush with Duane.

'Don't sweat it, treacle-trap – take her out for a posh cocktail afterwards. But please – keep her away from Sex On The Beach or a Slow Comfortable Screw!'

I'd laughed – well, it was smutty, of course I laughed – but I'd felt a bit weird. Of course they couldn't have known I knew about their bolshy bedmate, but to be honest I felt as though they were – what's the words – trying to 'buy my silence'.

The door in front of us opened and that's when I saw her – the Fox. She was walking towards us, and it seemed to me she was moving in slow motion – funnily enough, old Kimbo once told me she'd thought that the first time she saw me. She was every cliché about Oriental chicks rolled into one perfect size eight package, but instead of making you feel clumsy and gross like they usually do, she made me feel like standing up and cheering – she was that gorgeous. Course, she must've been twenty-three if she was a day, but after my doomed romance with Jailbait Lewis I could see the benefits of the older woman.

In short, she made me want to lick her face and kiss her feet and hold her down and see to her. To sum up – lust at first sight.

She stopped, frowned at a clipboard and called out, 'Susie?'

I didn't even think about it, I just jumped to my feet. 'Right here!' I was aware of Mum gaping at me, but she's used to me stealing the limelight, and why should the scene of her putative abortion be any different?

The Fox gave me a funny look and raised her eyebrow expertly, which always makes me feel a bit funny inside. 'But it says here—'

'PLEASE!' I hissed. 'I don't want to do this in public!'

She looked dubious, but turned anyway and walked towards a door marked DOCTOR – PRIVATE. There was a cardboard insert just beneath this:

DR MAXINE FOX

Ooh, perfecto! I practically hugged my bad self with sheer molten glee. I turned and gave Susie, who was by now staring at me saucer-eyed, the thumbs up.

'Where you going, Ave?' she whispered.

'Just got to – um – check out the, ah, the lie of the land!' I finished in a distracted rush, watching Dr Fox's back go through the doorway to her office. She turned, and she looked at me with just a *hint* of that arrogance which often seems to bubble under the compliant surface of Chinese birds – or perhaps that was just my fevered imagination . . .

'Susie?' she said, a bit stern like, and I straightened my pencil skirt and pushed Mum down as she tried to stand up. 'Get the weight off your feet!' I advised her over my shoulder as I tip-tapped into Dr Fox's lair. 'You're standing for two!' Too late I realized I'd played into her soppy old hands, and I was aware of her face crumpling again. Whatever!

Dr Fox was sitting down behind her desk when I got into her room, which was a shame as I'd been hoping for a good look at her legs.

'So you are . . .' She looked at her clipboard, then up at me. She did that eyebrow thing again. 'Susie Sweet. But there's surely some mistake. It says here you're thirty-five.'

'We live fast up Ravendene,' I said with a winning twinkle. The Fox frowned and I realized I'd got it the wrong way round. 'Good genes?' I said weakly. Then, in the corner, I espied a table-type thing covered in slippery paper. 'Shall I get my kit off, then?' I stood and began to unzip my skirt.

'PLEASE!' She stood up and shouted, but she was sort of smiling too. 'Let's cut to the chase, shall we? This is hardly the time or place for jokes.'

'I'm sorry.' I sat down. I'd tried the humorous approach, perhaps now it was time for a touch of tragedy.

'It's just that –' And here I made a little wobble come to my voice – 'My mum – Susie Sweet – she's never done anything like this before . . . she's a Catholic, innit . . .'

'Oh dear!' said the Fox sternly.

'Yeah, it sucks, dunnit!' I agreed readily.

'But if that's the case – excuse me, what *is* your name?'

'Maria Sweet. Well, Ave-Maria Sweet. But you can call me Sugar.'

'If that's the case, *Miss Sweet,* then why is your mother here?'

'Mental health,' I said, thinking on my feet. 'She reckons it's . . . ah, the spawn of the Devil. Like in that film. Cos she's, um, what's the word, *sinned.* And lapsed. And like, we all know it ain't Satan the Second, of course –' See the clever use of 'we' there, to bond me and the Fox into a team! – 'but there ain't no telling *her* that. And she says if she's made to have it, she's going to, like –' I knew I was being a bit naughty here, of course, but all's fair in love and war and stuff – 'um, *kill* it. So, you know, me being a good daughter and all that . . . well, I thought, might as well get it done by a professional.' Uh-oh, the Fox was looking daggers at me! 'I mean, might as well be hung for a sheep as a lamb. Not that I think it's killing . . . not like hanging . . . but on the other hand, you know, they deserve it most of the time.' She was looking at me absolutely baffled, I realized. 'Kiddy-fiddlers?' I added hopefully.

The Fox gave me a look that could have meant anything – fascination, lust, love – but, fair play, most likely meant that she thought I was an ocean-going prannet. So

I held up my hands, got to my feet and admitted defeat. 'Best leave it, yeah?'

'Yes. Best.' The Fox wasn't having any, that was plain to see, as she went to the door and opened it, looking at me sternly. Talk about 'a whopper a day keeps the doctor away'!

But a playa never says neva, and as I passed her I couldn't help whipping out a tampon, pulling off the cardboard and unrolling it in one graceful action – George Clooney's got nothing on me when it comes to smooth moves, I tell you! I grabbed a pen from the Fox's top pocket and scribbled my mobey number. Before she knew what had happened, I'd shoved it into the pocket, with her pen, *and* copped a quick backhand breaststroke into the bargain.

But she still wasn't having none, it seemed – and so neither was I, apparently. She shot me a look that would have put me straight into the freezer compartment, had I not been so hot-blooded, nudge nudge!

Joking apart, I knew when I was beat. So I licked my lips, batted my eyelashes and ran my hands casually down my breasts, as if smoothing my sweater, causing my nipples to pop out in a defeated, forlorn sort of way, natch.

But she still wasn't having none. She held the door open a fraction wider. As I walked away, I heard her voice, crisp and cross –

'Send your mother in, will you –'

I nodded, not even looking at her –

'*Sugar.*'

7

'And then she pushed me back on the table thing, right, and before you could say, "Do me three ways!" we were sliding about on that slippy paper. AND she looked like Lucy Liu!'

'What – right there in her office?' gasped Baggy at my feet, biting off a bit of cotton from the hem of my culottes. NOT one of my favourite outfits, to be honest.

'No – in *her* dreams!' sniggered Aggy, shoving him with his foot and me with his elbow. 'Admit, sherbet-dip – the nearest you got to experiencing the foxy doctor's bedside manner was when she asked you to help your mum on to a trolley!'

'OK . . .' I shrugged, 'but it's gonna happen, I just know it. She's playing a game with me, innit. You know . . . whatsit gratification . . . when you're not getting none—'

'*Deferred* gratification, saccharin-swizzler,' said Aggy. He snipped something off my sleeve and stood back, squinting. 'OK – it's a wrap!'

I gasped; I wasn't expecting my career as a muse to come to such a sudden end. 'That's the collection? It's finished?'

'The difficult bit – the designing is. Now all we have to do is make, show and market the gear – easy-peasy.' Aggy laughed. 'Just think, Bags will never have to kneel at your minging plates of meat ever again!'

'If only he could stop kneeling at yours too!' I shot back fast as lightning, and they both pinched me as one in two places. As well as the pain, I felt a warm glow: of belonging, of confidence, of self-esteem, of being valued for something other than sex, which had been all I'd known since I was thirteen or something. I was sad to think this might end.

'So . . . you won't need me any more?'

Aggy shook his head. 'Not unless you want to go back to skivvying for us.'

I shook my head, no way!

'As I thought . . . well, then I guess the answer is no, we don't need you to work for us any more.' He paused. 'So I guess you'll just have to settle for being a very special friend of ours, sugar-shack. How will that do?'

I threw my arms around him.

'Group hug!' shrieked Baggy, springing to his feet. As we stood there, I must admit that tears came to my eyes. And not *just* because Bags had stepped on my toes with the full force of his beloved body.

I walked home on air, feeling so good about myself, even though I was once more officially unemployed. I'd soon find something else. And what did I care – once a muse, always a muse!

My mood didn't change when I put my key in the door and walked into the kitchen. Jesus was lying on the sofa flicking through some tit-tastic lad mag and flipped me a friendly middle finger as I passed by. Swearers Three were still at it, it seemed, and even the twins 'singing', if that was the the word for it, couldn't get me down. I smiled as I watched them do a dance routine on the kitchen table, little Rajinder between them, performing their latest opus, 'The Little Shih-Tzu That Swore.'

'O little Shih-tzu you look so sweet
From the bow on your head to your four furry feet
But there's one thing about you that makes me sore
YOU'RE THE LITTLE SHIH-TZU THAT SWORE!'

Then, of course, came a list of all the bad words the delinquent dog could say. I looked at the twins swearing happily, their Punjabi mate between them, and I looked across at Mum, her back to a sink piled high with dirty dishes, laughing as she drank a watermelon Bacardi Breezer. I felt real pleased with her for pulling through her little adventure so cheerily – not to mention myself, for setting it up so well. We were like some warped sort of Waltons – only more fun. Personally, I was well proud of us.

Well, my love life seemed to be sorted – the foxy doctor was a sure thing, the way I saw it – my social life was sound – when the Baggy-Aggy collection came out, I was gonna be getting free goes at every bowling alley in town – but I still needed a rotten old job. And I still had this dream of getting out of Brighton, nabbing some private dick – heh heh! – and searching for Kim; sorry, REN. Well, both of 'em – Ren for Mum and Kim for me. But no need to tell her that right this minute!

So because Susie thought I was intending to get Ren back and do the brave single-mother stuff, she said that even when I got another job, I could still live at home rent free so's to be able to save – she's good like that, not too bright; I like that in a mother. Which is why I s'pose I could take or leave motherhood myself – there's just this whole side of yourself: intelligence, selfishness, enjoyment, that you're meant to kill off in order to be what people think of as a 'good' mother. But without them, so far as I could see, you weren't any longer a real person, just some sort of robot programmed to wipe asses and blow noses. Well, my mum's a Catholic and my husband's a Lutheran and I never really got a handle on either except that the first lot go in for a lot more confessing, but I do know one thing – if the good Lord had intended me to be a robot, I'd have a little panel on my chest that opened up so you could tell me what to do.

So that Thursday morning I bought the *Brighton Argus*, wrapped up warm and took it down to the beach for a read of the jobs. It's a good thing I'm not depressively inclined, or I would have drowned myself in the briny right there and then. The first job that caught my eye required a Chinese-speaking employee, which of course made me think of my foxy doc; get this – you had to be IT literate, and have at least two years experience! And for this, you got the skanky sum of £6 an hour. And they wonder why kids become ho's and drug dealers! It's a little word like

RESPECT – and ho's and dealers get a damn sight more respect from their clients, the way I see it, than 'decent' employees get from employers. At least they pay a decent rate for the goods!

I could've quite fancied working at the Spud-u-like (FRESH – HEALTHY – SATISFYING) but was put off by the fact that I knew I'd be the size of a house by the time I reached eighteen. And as for the call centre, which sported a smiley face by its logo – don't make me laugh! As has been pointed out from time to time, I'm a gobby cow, and within days of acting as a punchbag for some pissed-off consumer's ear-bashing, and not being allowed to answer back, I'd be gurning with rage, not grinning with glee.

Then I saw it –

**FOR A NEW CAREER THIS YEAR,
VISIT THE STANWICK AIRPORT CAREERS FAIR.**
Free admission. 10 a.m. to 8 p.m. Drivers – Retail –
Hospitality – Passenger Services – Flight Attendants –
Aircraft Grooming – Catering

I know this sounds dumb, right, but airports are really glamorous places to me. Maybe it's something to do with Mum never having taken us on holiday, but when I was about twelve, before I discovered shagging, sometimes I used to get the bus up to Stanwick and just sit in a Macky D's watching the planes flying off to who knows where. That line of white they leave behind . . . it's well my favourite sight in the world; it makes me think of freedom. And stands for all the stuff that goes towards making up one sweet life, the way I see it.

I could see myself in one of them cute little stewardess outfits, like Britney in 'Toxic', wiggling up and and down the aisles and pulling fit blokes into the toilets for a quickie. And when I found Kimmy – and Ren! – we could have all sorts of cheap holidays and free flights. It'd be well sweet . . .

And if I didn't find 'em, heck, I could always invite the foxy Maxine for a dirty weekend of Doctors and Nurses. Got to have a Plan B. Or in my case, a Plan XXX.

So next day I was up Stanwick like a shot. But, to cut to the chase – or rather, to the free flight that never happened – it wasn't to be, my stewardess fantasy. Strike one – I wasn't eighteen or above. Strike two – no passport. And strike three – no GCSEs. I mean, like they're going to be REALLY useful, for pouring drinks and wearing a tight skirt! However, I WAS old enough, English enough and dumb enough to be an airport cleaner, as it soon turned out at the Stanwick Airport Careers Fair. Yes, all right, I KNOW! But it wasn't just being a cleaner; it was being part of an airport. It was part of getting away.

So here's our schedule. There's five crews, working rotating shifts – cleaning toilets, departure and arrival lounges and check-in areas; clearing rubbish, emptying ashtrays, wiping tables, vacuuming baggage-claim and check-in halls, cleaning check-in desks and lots of offices. I'm like the youngest on our crew, then there's this pair of

Goths in their late twenties, early thirties – the state of them! Call themselves the Dracules, but I happen to know that their real name's Lambie. They spend most of their time bickering and you kinda get the impression Drina/Katie would be happy to bin the black lace and throw on a cute sundress but Drew/Josh still insists on living the Goth dream or the nightmare, or whatever. Still, they can be a laugh when they want to be.

Then there's Mrs Tribbley – late fifties, walks around wearing a badge saying DO NOT RESUSCITATE and talking about her 'imminent' death as though it was a date with him out of Hard-Fi, though she looks as fit as a vet's vole to me. There's Kathleen and Kathryn, mid-thirties, who basically hate each other and engage in competitive cleaning – if one's on her hands and knees scrubbing sick off a toilet floor, the other will make sure she gets her head right down the bowl, no gloves, nothing to kneel on – hardcore. You should see the time I take to clean the toilet mirrors when all this is going on!

Then there's the two daddies of the pack – Nev and Navdeep. Nev's an ex-docker from Shoreham and Nav's this cool Sikh with a turban and all that, and sometimes he lets us touch his dagger! They're kind to us, but they're very much a self-contained pair, spending most of their breaks doing Sudoku and trying to force us to do them too, 'To keep your brains working,' as Nav would say sternly. What's he mean, keep! – most of us, they never started. Specially the luggage guys who just play football all the time.

So it smells and it's slow and it's hardly the stuff dreams are made of, but there's a few perks. First, the security staff have to search you every time you go in and out of the lounges, and some of them are well fit. And second is this mystery boy, about my age, who keeps himself to himself and spends all his spare time with his squeegee, but he's just about the prettiest thing you ever saw. Asif, I think his name is. And one of these days, not long from now, if he hangs around too long in the cloakrooms after home-time, he's going to get some Sweet-smooching. A Sugar-shagging, even.

Yes, I KNOW! What do I want – boy or girl, Indian or Chinese? Seems like I just can't make up my mind these days. But whatever, it's all sweet.

8

Cute as a Christmas puppy or not, I didn't just want to jump feet first into a relationship – or even a sex-thang – with some cute immigrant kid who cleaned out karzies for a living. Don't forget, I was still walking on air, or at least some invisible catwalk, from my recent reign as Baggy and Aggy's muse. Though my part in their next world-conquering collection was finished in practical terms, I still couldn't shake the notion that there might be some sort of modelling job for me when the clothes were finally good to go.

I was standing in the restroom phoning them on their landline for the nth time that day – having been texting them and trying their mobeys all week – suggesting we get together, when I heard the door go behind me. I turned around and there was Asif – his mouth was like a kiss, I thought immediately, and as he looked at me it was like I could see birthday candles in his eyes. I closed my phone, walked across to him and, reaching behind him, I closed the door softly. Yes, I KNOW what I said, but rules were made to be broken. Especially your own. And especially ESPECIALLY if there might be a decent shag as a result.

'Knock knock,' I whispered in his ear.

He stared at me, terrified.

'Say "Who's there?",' I prompted him.

'Who is there!' His eyes went really big – big mistake, as it only made him more perve-worthy.

'Asif,' I purred.

'Asif –' He pointed at himself and smiled nervously.

'Say "Asif Who?",' I instructed.

He laughed, finally realizing I meant him no harm. Hmm, well, not in a VIOLENT way. Unless he struggled, of course. 'Asif who!'

'As-if-I-wouldn't-snog-you,' I whispered in his ear. He turned his head slowly – I kept mine still; we were eye to eye and mouth to mouth. And by the look in his eye, and the way his lips parted, I knew we were speaking the same language, all right.

But as I said, I wasn't about to throw my future away on some tasty toilet-tender. Play it as cool and sweet as ice cream, that's the Sugar-shock. I held my phone up to his mouth.

'Put your number in. But kiss it first.'

'Kiss . . .?'

'It's a Sussex custom. "Silly Sussex", they call us. Cos we get a rush out of doing daft things. You know what a rush is, don't you, Asif?'

'When people hurry – they rush—'

'Na, not that type. The fun kind.' I pushed the phone against his lush lips and he winced. 'You want to have fun, don't you – not just clean out toilets all your life? You're too beautiful to be doing a crap job like this . . .'

He shook his head. 'No . . . YOU are beautiful – I am . . .'

'You're gorgeous.' I put the phone in his hand. 'Put your number in –'

I watched his lovely dark face as he did it, wondering if he was blushing or not. He handed it back to me.

'That's right,' I told him. 'So now I've got your number, we can have fun.'

'Tonight? When we finish work? We go out?'

Why not? Wasn't like I had any other hot date lined up when I finished going berserk with the Cillit Bang, was it? I opened my mouth to give him instructions.

Then my phone rang.

I checked it – Baggy and Aggy's landline. And seeing it, I snapped back into reality – MY reality. A place where people lived in big white houses and did creative things – not cleaned toilets and ate at Burger King before a quick fumble by the bins round the back.

I gave Asif a quick dismissive smile – 'Not today, kid – I'll call you sometime' – and a good view of my coldest shoulder as I turned away to take the call.

'Hiya!' I squealed into the phone. 'How's it hanging!' Behind me I heard the door close quietly, and if a door could sound sad, it certainly did.

'Pretty good, last time I looked,' someone sniggered. But it wasn't B or A.

'Who's this?'

'It's Duane, Shugs – Duane Trulocke.'

'Oh, right.' I couldn't help feeling a bit hurt that my mates were still obviously doing whatever they were doing with Duane, when they hadn't had any time for me. 'They still screwing you, then?'

'Yeah, I s'pose.' There was a pause. 'But not just me. You want to meet up?'

An hour later I was watching Duane walk through the door of the Macky D's in the Western Road. I could tell straight away that something was up, because usually he walked like he'd just done your brother and was on his way to do your mother – dead cocky. But now he was walking like he'd just done your budgie, and then let it out the window into the bargain – real shifty, like he didn't know how to break the awful news.

He sat down opposite me and pinched a chip. I pushed my tray towards him. 'Go on, have the lot! I'm not touching 'em, I know where your fingers have been!'

'Same to you. How come you got McNuggets? Thought Filet-o-Fish was more your speed,' he sniggered.

I hate that – the way everyone knows about me and Kizza. It's like I'm labelled for life – DYKE! KEEP OFF! Another reason why I should bag Asif. But then, it's like another label – two teenage toilet cleaners copping off together! Dead depressing. That's why I needed to climb out of my 'box', so to speak – score the smart, exotic Dr Fox, or better still some really hot creative bloke. Like Baggy and Aggy – only not gay. Or a minger. Or a couple. You know what I mean!

'Spit out it,' I said coldly. 'And I don't mean the chips. Haven't you got something better to do like, ooh, I don't know, perving over some fit bird that's been like a sister to you when she's spread-eagled on six square foot of Baco-Foil with her defences down?'

He didn't say anything, just got out his phone. 'Want to show you something – because you WERE like a sister to me, cos you knew I didn't have no proper family. You were dead kind. Even when Jesus and me done that thing with the superglue and your tampon that time—'

'Spare me the gory details,' I said hurriedly. Sitting in McDonald's with a rent boy, discussing sticky fun with tampons from times past, having just clocked off from my cleaning job, was hardly the glamorous life I was cut out for, at the risk of sounding snobbish. 'Just tell me the big news and let me finish my Fruit 'n' Yogurt Parfait in peace.'

He got out his phone, fiddled with it and pushed it slowly across the table to me, screen downwards, looking furtively around as he did so. As I reached out for it I had the most horrible feeling that I was never going to feel the same about B&A again after looking at it. I put my hand over it and pushed it back towards him.

'Put it away, Duane. I don't want to see what they've done to you.'

'Do you want to see what they've done to YOU, though?'

He pushed the phone back and this time I picked it up.

The first picture showed my Princess dress on a mannequin. Only it wasn't the Princess dress the way it had been described to me. It was still short and sleeveless but it wasn't black silk – it was made out of a black rubbish sack, with glitter splashed randomly over it. And the label across the dummy's face said, in big black capitals, WHITE-TRASH TINKERBELL.

I looked up at Duane. He may only have been fifteen, and a little prick of a bum-chum rent boy, but I suddenly wanted him to put his arms around me and tell me everything would be all right. Instead he shrugged and said, 'I'm sorry, Shugs. But I just thought you should know –'

I nodded, and hit the button. Next up was my beautiful micro-mini skating skirt with attached knickers, which was meant to have been in lush red velvet – with matching muff! But now it was in a horrible check – even worse than Burberry! – and as for the muff . . . well, you can guess what *that* was made to resemble. The label on this one said PRAM-FACED PRICKTEASE. My sight was a bit blurry by this time, but I noted that the next dress had pregnancy tests hanging off the hem and was called LATE AGAIN! Then there was PIKEY PRINCESS – a princess at last! – and CHIPSHOP CHIC.

Then I came to the final shot. It was the culottes. I've always hated culottes anyway. But these – these were bright yellow, with gurgling babies printed all over them. And a trickle of blood running down from the crotch. It was called MUM'S ABORTION.

I couldn't believe it. My friends. MY FRIENDS . . .

Duane took his phone back from me gently. 'You didn't know about none of this, did you.'

I shook my head, no.

'But you were modelling for them for ages—'

'They put these white material things on you – "toiles", they're called. They help them get the outline right – then they cut it on the proper material . . . that way there's no waste . . .' The fact that I knew this thing which I'd been perfectly OK not knowing seemed to sum up for some dumb freaking reason every dumb freaking thing I'd hoped for, and I suddenly saw how I'd been SO fooled by these bastards into believing that I could be something I wasn't, when all I'd ever be was a chav. A chipshop-chic, pram-faced pricktease, white-trash, late-again CHAV – worrying about her mum's abortion! They lied to me, and they gave me money, and they dressed me up and let me look into their mirrors – and I saw a princess. But those mirrors were evil fairground mirrors, it turned out, because where I saw a princess, the rest of the world just saw a pikey. And always would, because of everything about me, from my blood to my postcode.

I began to stuff cold chips into my mouth then, just more and more and more, until they started to fall out, because of course I couldn't swallow because my throat had closed up, because I was crying.

'Ria! RIA!' Duane sounded really shocked. Yeah, I know – I never cried! But then, I'd never been made to look ten types of twat in one go by a pair of giggling paedos, had I! Through my veil of tears I saw him get up from his seat and then I felt his arms go round me and pull me gently up from my seat. I made a half-hearted attempt at shaking him off – it was all wrong, me being comforted by a boy.

'Leave me 'lone – want my parfait!' I protested.

'No! – come on! – you've got a rep, you can't be seen blubbing in here!'

I let him manhandle, or rather boyhandle, me out, and we walked without speaking up North Street to the corner of West Street, the long hill of clubs and pubs that leads to the seafront, often referred to by the local police as 'Little Beirut'. As we walked past the scene of many a conquest and catfight, I couldn't help thinking how bloody 'ironic' – thanks, Kim! – it was that I had had so many run-ins here with some of the toughest types in town, boys and girls both, yet in all that pushing and shoving I had never once been made to cry. And now I was in floods because of a pair of namby-pamby middle-aged frock-makers.

And it struck me that I'd been *so much stronger* before I knew what irony was. Maybe you're just better off not knowing certain things.

'It's called "The Council Couture Collection",' Duane said apologetically after a few minutes. 'I would have told you before. Only I thought at first you might have been in on the joke.'

'No. I was just the punchline.' A black rubbish bag taunted me with my dreams of glory and I kicked it viciously. It spilt its guts everywhere – a bit like I had with those *bastards*.

'I heard them talking about it – they said they was sick of making frocks for thick rich footballers' wives and this was their experimental collection,' he said helpfully.

'I'LL BLOODY EXPERIMENT ON THEM!' I screeched, stopping dead still. 'I'll take a pair of their freaking huge pattern-cutting scissors and a tube of your superglue, and I'll make them the first two-faced, two-headed gaylord on earth to have two crinkle-cut bum-holes, THAT'S what I'll do –'

But then I realized that there was no point in making a minger-monster out of them – who'd notice the difference, for one? However, there was SOMETHING I could do with scissors and superglue that would make a LOT of difference to their lovely jubbly quality of life, the twisted trollops . . .

I grabbed Duane and shoved him against the glass front of the amusement arcade at the bottom of West Street. 'You got a key to their place?'

'I can nick one—'

'You know what date they're showing their crap collection?'

'I can find out—'

'Come on then!' I grabbed his hand and pulled him across the road towards the sea. Car horns shrieked in protest, but I was used to that; I didn't give a damn about the clamour or the anger that followed in my wake – bring it on! The thing was that I had a plan, and I was back on my feet, teetering down the shingle in high heels, dragging a laughing Duane after me. MY LIFE!

9

Well, it was a somewhat different Sugar who clocked in at Stanwick next day, Saturday, and while I can't exactly claim that I embraced my mop and bucket as though they were him off of T4, or even my passport to a better life, I *did* look at them like there were a pair of old – what's the word – *adversaries*, that's right, who had to be faced before I could move on to anything else.

Another difference was that I was no longer looking down my nose at young Asif. Instead I was looking down my cleavage at him, grinning like a loon, while he failed to notice me and instead nodded seriously at what Navdeep was saying.

'See, kid, what the English are only just starting to understand is that your extreme Muslim didn't come here to get freedom from persecution – he came here to get the freedom to persecute everybody else! Now what were you telling me about your church in Pakistan—'

'Ooh, are you religious?' I asked brightly. 'My –' I was about to say, 'My husband's a Lutheran,' but then I reckoned it probably wasn't the greatest chat-up line in the world. 'My, that's good!' I swerved.

'My parents – we're Christians,' said Asif proudly.

'Onward Christian soldiers!' I said fiercely, giving a clenched fist salute.

Asif looked appalled.

'I'll leave you kids to your theological discussion,' laughed Nav, getting up. 'I dunno, Maria, though – you Brits and your precious multiculturalism. It's all sweetness and light when it's curry houses and late opening corner shops, but it's not so much fun when it's honour-killings and book-burning, is it! Or murdering the rest of us. Ask him!' He inclined his head towards Asif. 'I can't help thinking about what my mum says when she sees 'em marching about, having the screaming abdabs – "I came here from the Punjab because I wanted to live in *England* – not because I want to live in a multicultural country. If I'd wanted to live in one of them, I'd have stayed in India!".' And with that he went to whup Nev's aye-ss over a new Sudoku.

I looked at Asif. He was staring at me with shining eyes, both eager and wary. I held his look, rolled it around a bit, and bounced it right back at him with bells on. 'So, we on for this thea – thea – this logical discussion, then?' I twinkled.

He nodded. 'I am always free when not at work – apart from church, of course.'

'Of course,' I agreed angelically. 'Me too.' I paused then, got right to the point. 'So, like, you want to get some, ASAP?'

'Absolutely.' He took my hand in his, and as I looked down at it, I got this warm glow right in the core of my stomach. At first I thought it was because of the colour thing, the racial harmony thing, and I felt well proud of myself.

But then a split second later I realized it was because our hands, joined like that, looked like a Benetton ad. And that made me feel like a model – as near as I was ever gonna get to being one now. Which reminded me . . .

But pleasure before business! 'So when you want to do it?'

'Tomorrow morning?'

'Wahey! – you're eager, aren't you! Well, we're not working till the evening – and I guess it would be sort of special not to do it here for the first time . . .'

'Yes, I think so. Though of course, wherever there are two of one mind, it's always appropriate.'

Boy, was he learning fast or what!

'Though ideally there would be three or more of us –' He caught me by the shoulders and stared at me full on, his eyes searching my face as though he thought he'd find the final rollover number there. Which in a way was the truth, I s'pose, if you want to be smutty about it.

'Steady on, tiger!' I was getting well hot and bothered now, as a vivid image of me, Asif and Dr Foxy rolling around under the Palace Pier came into my head. Bit parky for it, though – still, just have to stay extra-close for warmth!

'You live in Brighton – would you like to do it there?' He was well animated now, getting more excited by the minute!

'Well – where do you live?'

'Crawley.'

'No, I definitely don't want to do it there!'

71

We laughed, and for the first time, I didn't feel like he was a foreigner.

'Shall I come to your house at nine o'clock?'

'Hang about!' It's not like Mum was a racist – I mean, look at me! It was a warm day in Sussex when I was born, obviously – you don't get a black-haired, olive-skinned baby from sleeping with the boy next door, obviously. But there's caffè latte and there's double espresso, and these things can make all the difference when they're banging on your front door – with a view to banging your daughter – at the crack of dawn. 'Why don't I meet you at the station? Then we can just stroll down and stop where the fancy takes us . . .'

'What a lovely idea, Maria.' He looked genuinely moved, which never hurts a girl's ego, I find. I could have sworn there were actual tears in his eyes! 'It *should* be spontaneous – as the spirit moves us!'

'Couldn't agree more!' I stroked his lovely face and planted a light, teasing kiss on his lips, making him blush, bless him! Boy – isn't it great when you find yourself singing from the same hymn sheet!

So that's how come, at nine thirty next morning, I was sitting in a Baptist Church in Hove praising the Lord. To add insult to injury, I didn't recognize one of the hymns – all intro, no tune! On the plus side, the vicar – or 'pastor' as they called him – was quite fit, as well as the congregation; lots of lush ethnics there, but no sign of the foxy Maxine.

She struck me as the bolshy non-believer sort, anyway. And of course she was an abortionist!

I sneaked a sideways peek at the gorge God-botherer who'd got me into this as I mouthed the words to one of the tuneless wonders, and he shot me the sort of smile that made it all worthwhile. We finished the alleged hymn and sat down, and bugger me if the pastor didn't start banging on about how much he 'desired' his wife! The irony! And here was I, heading for Nunsville on the No-Sex Express!

'Stand up, Moira!' yelled the pastor lustily. We all rubber-necked like crazy before our eyes came to rest on this pretty boring broad in that sorta late twenties–early thirties zone, where it's all going pear-shaped, i.e. RIGHT ON TO THE HIPS! She was looking down at her feet – though with hips like that it'd be a wonder if she could see them, come to think of it. 'Yes, that's my wife – Moira!'

We made sort of approving noises – even me. Well, it seemed a bit bad to shout 'Oi! – Cankles!' in a church, which was the first thing that came into my mind to be honest.

'Moira – tell the people – do I give you flowers?'

Moira mumbled something.

'Speak up, Moira! – TELL the people!'

Moira cleared her throat. 'Yes!'

'And tell the people, Moira – do I give you flowers because I feel I SHOULD give you flowers?' – dramatic pause! – 'OR BECAUSE I DESIRE YOU?'

Moira mumbled something.

'TELL THE PEOPLE, MOIRA! TELL *ALL* THE PEOPLE!'

'BECAUSE YOU DESIRE ME!' Moira yelled.

All around us people applauded. But Asif and I looked at each other amazed, then away to keep from choking with laughter. In that moment I became totally determined to have him. Even more determined than when I'd got a real close eyeful of the back of his neck once while we were queuing up to get our Toilet Duck. Or that time when I'd been pissed on gin miniatures the Dracule-Lambies had smuggled off a plane, given the lads in Security a quick flash of the puppies fighting to get out of their Wonderbra kennel and noticed that there was a lot more going on in young Asif's trousers than his butter-wouldn't-melt expression would imply. Forget butter, you could have melted brass down there from what I'd glimpsed before he scurried out of the rest-room. It's funny how sharing a laugh, or better still suppressing one, can bring you closer to someone than a blow job will. Funny ha-ha, funny peculiar and funny quite-sad really, if you think about it.

But as I think I've said before, too much thinking's well bad for the complexion. So I just squeezed Asif's hand and relished the feeling of him squeezing back. An old disco song Mum used to play a lot came back to me –

'There'll be twenty minutes of squeezing
Twenty minutes of pleasing
TWENTY MINUTES OF BLOWING MY TOP!'

I went 'Ooh . . .' quite loud, without meaning to, just thinking about me and Asif eventually having our 'Happy Hour', so to speak, and wouldn't you know it the pervy old pastor fixed me with a beady eye!

'Miss!' he only goes and yells. 'Do you hear what I'm saying?'

'Um, yeah!' I yelled back, hoping he'd leave me alone and pick on someone else if I agreed with him.

'Listen! From the mouths of babes!' he screeched – bit personal, I thought, drawing attention to my looks in church! 'And this is what the Lord wants from us – not for us to worship Him through duty – BUT TO WORSHIP HIM THROUGH DESIRE! So now, let us SING to him our final hymn – with DESIRE!'

With this the congregation went ape, cheering and 'Amen!'-ing like they'd just won the Cup. With the exception of Asif and me, that is – as one, we stood up and legged it out of there. Outside on the pavement we cracked up, hurrying down the hill to the seafront gasping for breath. It wasn't till we were sitting on the beach looking out to sea that we spoke.

'Well, that was a laugh and a half!' I lit a gasper and offered him one. 'Wunnit!'

He shook his head. 'Yes, it was. But church is not the place for giggles. Joy, yes, of course. But not giggles.'

'Well . . . I'm sorry,' I offered. Any indignity for the chance of a decent beach-shag!

'No . . . I don't blame you – why should you not find fun in the foolishness of those who should know better?'

He picked up a pebble and tossed it out to sea. 'All that talk of desire – I didn't like that too much. We were meant to be worshipping God – not his wife, nice as she may be.'

'Yeah – why don't they get a room!' I agreed. And I meant it – but I also thought it was a good way to turn the talk from the holy to the hoochy, if you get my drift. I lay back on elbows and looked up at him from under my lashes. 'Come to that . . . why don't we . . .'

But old Asif wasn't having none – and neither was I, by the looks of it. He picked up a handful of pebbles and let them fall through his fingers; I arched my back and imagined them as kisses falling on my body. He frowned at them as they fell; I imagined him frowning down at me as I went to work on him, before the downturned mouth turned first up in an incredulous smile, and then into a pure O of bliss . . .

'I keep looking for the right church, but I cannot seem to find it. The other week, at an otherwise excellent Catholic church near Fulking, there was a sign up saying PLEASE MIND YOUR HANDBAGS!'

'Bloody pikeys,' I agreed. 'My mum's one,' I added in case he thought I was prejudiced.

'I am too impatient,' – so am I, mate, so am I! – 'where instead, I should be grateful for the opportunity just to worship in peace.' He looked up at me, his eyes narrowed against the sun and something else. 'You know what I mean?'

'No – why don't you tell me?'

'Later.' He laid back then, but he still wasn't relaxed.

Well, he was laying on pebbles. But you know, I just got the feeling he never would be, not even if he was laying back on a hammock made of hardcore cloud, hitched between two solid old stars.

Well, I knew he was stressing, and I felt for him – I really did. But, on the other hand, surely this was the moment when more than ever he needed to, um, *empower* himself. So, to help him, I straddled him in one smooth move.

AND HE PUSHED ME OFF!

'Jeez, man! Don't BE that guy!' I sat up and rubbed my left elbow where it was skinned.

'Maria! – SUGAR! – I am SO sorry!' He grabbed my arm and stared at my elbow. He looked horrified. 'WHAT HAVE I DONE!'

'It's no big –' I started, then thought better of it. It wouldn't hurt him to feel a bit guilty – I might even get a shag out of it, or even a bag of chips! 'It HURRRTS!' I howled.

'Oh, MARIA!' He threw both arms around me and pulled me close, tucking the top of my head under his chin. It felt nice – pure, but sort of pervy too. 'I know what it is to be hurt – and now I have hurt you! I am worthless!'

'Steady on!' A guilt trip was one thing, but having him immobilized by self-loathing was a whole nother speed-bump. Actions speak louder than words in my experience, so I held up my poor elbow right next to his mouth. 'If you really want to make it up to me, kiss it better.'

'Is another English custom – like when I have to kiss

77

your phone?' I wouldn't have bet on it, but I thought I could hear a smile in his voice.

'Yeah.'

'Is Silly Sussex thing?'

'That's right.' I held his gaze.

'Really?' And now he really did smile, with his voice and his mouth and his eyes and everything. He kissed my elbow, ever so gently. 'I wonder what I must kiss next . . .'

Reader, I showed him!

10

Well, it wasn't exactly pillow talk, what happened afterwards, but then the pebbles weren't exactly pillows. They were hard and they hurt my head – but not as much as the things Asif told me. I didn't know much about Pakistan apart from that you're not meant to call them 'Pakis' – as I'd pointed out to little Rajinder. But it turns out that some of them do much worse things to their own people than call them names – much worse.

It started so hopefully, our 'afterglow' – heh heh! – conversation: 'D'you know what love is, Maria? Shall I tell you?' – but it ended up with me blubbing like a baby there on the beach, with Asif holding me and rocking me like one. Then when I'd calmed down he got his hanky and cleaned me up and walked me to the bus stop and waited with me till it came. It was still only early afternoon, but when I got home I went straight to my room and got into bed – luckily everyone was out – and just lay there staring at the ceiling, thinking about what Asif had said. Turned out the love he was talking about was his love for Jesus, of all people (now that's what even I call serious competition), and how just wanting to show this love, by being a Christian, had led to the most unbelievable stuff happening to his lot back in Pakistan – this was apparently what Navdeep had meant when he said, 'Ask him!'

*

Well, in a way I'm glad I did and in another way I wish I hadn't. I've never been that big on religion – when my bastard ex, Mark, used to start banging on about Lutheranism, I used to do this mental thing of trying to calculate and name all the people I'd done the nasty with, which made me look like I was listening and concentrating really hard on what he was saying. Admittedly it wasn't very supportive, but then, as it turned out, neither was he. Anyway, it was just words, Mark's religion – he could go on about being a Lutheran till he grew wings and flew, and nobody was gonna get on his case about it. So why bother getting all het up about it?

With Asif it was different. What I said about actions speaking louder than words – well, over in Pakistan, your words can get you killed. It's not something I'd ever given a lot of thought to, politics and that. Well, I mean I'd seen them Muslims on the TV parading about having hissy fits and thought how mad can they get? But from what Asif told me, when they get to be the government they can get a whole lot madder.

Where Asif came from. I shook my head from side to side on the pillow, like I was trying to shake out all the things I now knew. The thoughts that kept pushing to the front of the queue and hitting me again and again were the eight Christian girls he'd told me about who were taken off a bus and gang-raped while the Muslim girls were left untouched – the ten-year-old Christian girl raped as 'punishment' for the war in Iraq – the nine-year-old girl tortured and sexually abused and beaten with a cricket bat because she was a Christian. Girls like my little sisters. Then there were the priests shot dead, the churches destroyed by hand grenades and fire, the people burned alive as they sang hymns. And as Asif explained, because most of Pakistan is Muslim, and the government's Islamic, nobody does sod all to help the Christians, basically.

After he'd told me all this stuff, I was so grateful he'd got away that I couldn't even speak, just kept saying in my head, 'Thank you, thank you!' over and over.

Not that I think we should let just anybody in, mind you – I wouldn't trust the sodding Albanians as far as I could throw 'em.

So in a bit, to break the silence, I said, 'I don't like Albanians. Do you?'

He held me away from him and gave me this really sad look. 'Maria. If you had seen what prejudice can do, as it has in my country, you wouldn't never say that you disliked people just because of their nationality.'

'I don't dislike them cos of their nationality – I dislike 'em cos they look at me funny,' I pointed out. He tried to frown, but I could tell he was trying not to laugh. 'Gotcha!' I couldn't help teasing.

'Yes. Yes, you have.' He looked very serious. 'I don't know if that's going to be much fun for you, though.'

'You're joking!' I held his face in my hands. 'Look at you!'

'Yes. Look at me.' He held his arm out against mine. 'And then look at you.'

'Like a Benetton ad, innit!'

'Or a warning.' He frowned. 'To stick to your own kind.'

'What?' I laughed. 'Why would I want to do a thing like that?' It was true, I'd never stuck to my own kind; posh Kim, religious Mark, foxy Oriental Maxine if this thing with Asif didn't work out, fingers crossed! No, there's something a bit wussy about sticking to your own kind – like you're trying to blend in with the crowd. And let's face it, I couldn't do that if I wanted to. Which I don't.

'Because it's safe—'

'WE'RE safe.' I kissed him. 'You wanna learn the proper meaning of that word if you're gonna live here. We're safe. And sweet.'

It got all nice and sexy again after that, and as I touched him I felt like I was stroking away all the things that had hurt him. But now I was lying in bed by myself, with all that silence like a big blank white screen for me to see all those pictures on, hear all those screams against.

I was grateful for once when I heard the front door open and those little freaks my sisters coming in. I didn't even mind when they started their caterwauling. Then the words came through, loud and clear, and they sounded so stark, so sad, so savage this time – not funny any more –

'Then a third girl, called Rajinder, from the Paki shop –'

I pulled the pillow over my head and cried.

But in my experience, there's nothing that gives sadness a

good kicking faster than a good revenge plan, so when I wasn't giving old Asif a big old dose of sexual healing, heh heh, I was plotting the downfall of those dirty frockers Baggy and Aggy. As I'd already established with young Master Trulocke, a key could be nicked and a collection date could be established and, even better, a pair of scissors and a tube of Superglue can be had in any old corner shop, which frankly I find shocking. I mean, any old champion chav, pram-faced pricktease with a bad attitude and a bit of loose change could get hold of them! But hey, if they're selling, I'm sure as hell buying!

So I was sitting in the rest room during my break one day trying to decide whether or not I was going to be flying solo on this one. Duane had already made it clear he wasn't up for it, moaning like an old woman that he 'owed me one' so he'd lift a key, but on the other hand – I loved this! – he 'owed them too'. Well, they'd certainly treated him to plenty of roasts!

I couldn't ask Asif to be my apprentice either cos of his high moral standards – which admittedly were a little less 'rigorous' since I'd seen fit to take him in 'hand'.

It was at times like this I really missed old Kizza. She'd been a bit of a boffin at first, but I soon had her seeing things my way – crooked! Like that time we maxed her mum's credit card after Kiz caught her doing the dirty with Dale the decorator and we knew there wasn't gonna be no comeback. Course in the end we'd pushed the partners-in-crime thing a bit far, but it was good while it lasted.

So I was just resigning myself to going it alone when

the Dracules walked in, arguing as usual. Their problem is that they're Goths who grew up rather than died young, and now they're having to handle all the shit that getting old entails. Katie's rather more willing to do this than Josh, because she's someone's mum now – a tot who at the age of eighteen months still doesn't have a name because she wants to call it Luke and he wants to call it Bela. Which they were rowing about as they walked in.

'Isn't it bad enough he's with my parents eight hours a day, four days a week, while we're working our fangs off in this dump!' Josh, sorry, Drew was shrieking. It's true, they do have fangs – little implants, they are, quite cool if you like that sort of thing. 'My dad's a sodding VICAR, for Hades' sake! You want our boy to be called LUKE LAMBIE?! Yeah, that sounds like a real son of Satan!'

'BUT HE'S NOT THE SON OF SATAN!' Katie/Drina yelled back. 'He's OUR son! And Luke's a lovely name!' She looked embarrassed when she saw me. 'Oh – sorry, Sugar, didn't know you were here.'

'Don't worry – it's an interesting debate,' I shrugged. I was starting to think that the thrill-seeking, devil-worshipping side of the Family Dracule might be up for a bit of wanton destruction, and that I wouldn't have to run amok all on my lonesome. I took two Red Bulls out of the fridge and pulled a half-bottle of cheap voddy from my bag. 'Workers' playtime?' I grinned, waggling it at them.

Well, I've never known a Goth not to automatically take the bait. It's got to be CHEAP vodka, mind you – I've actually seen old Goths at parties turn down Absolut if there's any Vladivar going – and preferably it's got to be a half bottle, not a big one. It reminds them of their glory days I guess – first shag in a graveyard, first trip to Camden Market, first piercing. The good old/young days, when your Celtic neck tattoo didn't look like a turkey with a patterned scarf on!

'Cheers, Shugs!' grinned Josh, flopping down on to a chair and accepting my proffered gift. He glared at Katie. 'I s'pose you're too pure for this now!'

'Oh, shut your fang-hole!' she snapped, grabbing it off him and pouring a healthy slug into her tinny before handing it back. She took a deep drink and sighed. 'Got a fag, Shugs?'

I gave her one. 'So.' I lit it. 'What's eating you two kids? Tell Sugar.'

Katie hesitated, then plunged right in. 'Basically, Sugar, it's a problem that's not going to concern you for ages – how old are you?'

'Seventeen.'

'KATIE! It's not ever going to concern her, is it! She's not a fucking Goth, and never has been, whereas US . . .' I swear his lip trembled; these Antichrists, they're all a bunch of wusses! 'It's been our whole LIVES – it brought us together, that time when our piercings went septic and we had to wait all night at A and E at Brighton General, d'you remember?'

They both go all misty-eyed at this, so I wait respectfully for a nanosecond before enquiring politely, 'So – what happened?'

'I'll tell you, shall I, Sugar?' Katie glared at Josh, baring her fangs in the process. 'We had a Goth wedding – on the Vampire Ride at Chessington – no probs. We had a honeymoon in Transylvania – it rained all the time, but still no worries. We came back – got a Goth pet –'

'– a bat called Boris –' put in Josh brightly.

'– and we even found him a Goth vet!'

I nodded seriously, trying not to laugh. 'So – what's the problem?'

'My point exactly, Sugar,' put in Josh smugly. 'There wasn't one –'

'TILL WE HAD LUKE!'

'BELA!'

'Listen to him, Sugar,' Katie implored. 'Imagine his first day at school and he's called Bela! The kids aren't going to hang around waiting for him to spell it and point out that it's not a girl's name. They're just going to get in there and bully him!'

'Would that be a bad thing, then?' I asked innocently. Should have seen the evils they gave me! – two hearts were suddenly beating as one again, thanks to Sugar!

'What on earth do you mean, Maria?' says Katie, well posh suddenly.

'Well, you're Goths, innit – you like it when stuff goes wrong – and you like evil – so like . . . well, bullying's evil, innit?'

'Are you honestly suggesting we want Bela –'

'– LUKE! –'

'– our CHILD to be bullied, Maria?'

'But you like death, you lot!' I moaned defensively. I didn't like the way this was going! 'And death's a lot worse than having your head stuffed down the bog, face it!' But I just couldn't seem to bring myself to back away from the shovel, and proceeded to dig an even bigger hole for myself. 'So like . . . you know . . . while we're on the subject, I've always been curious – when someone a Goth loves gets really sick, like INCURABLY, do they like it? And if, you know, the worst comes to the worst – I mean, what are your feelings then?' I made an all-out attempt to claw back some goodwill as the Dracules stared at me in absolute – well, I was going to say 'horror', but that's a term of approval to them, innit! I took a deep breath. 'What I mean is, do you lot only like death and funerals in theory – or in practice too?'

Well, I finally hit pay dirt with this one because they stopped glaring and looked ashamed instead. I was mystified till Mr Dracule enlightened me.

'I know what you're thinking, Sugar –'

'Really?' I didn't!

'Yeah!' He sniggered in a self-loathing sort of way. 'It's like we said earlier – you've got the gift of youth – you look at us and you see sad old has-beens – or never-wases –'

'No!' I shrieked, probably with more force than was absolutely necessary – I just found it such a downer seeing the Dracules wallow in self-pity. 'I don't think that a bit.' I was starting to think on my feet now, and I could definitely see a way for both the Dracs and myself to come out of this with benefits. 'I never think of you two as old – not like the other people here – not like Kath and Kath and Mrs Tribbley – or Nav and Nev even –' They looked surprised and pleased at this; they both smiled broadly, showing their sweet little fangs. 'In fact, I was going to ask you if you fancied having a bit of a last – walk on the wild side, I s'pose you could call it. Every great duo goes out in a big way, don't they, before they hang up their – whatsits.'

'Holsters?' asked Josh.

'Could be!' I smiled. 'Thelma and Louise, Bonnie and Clyde . . . um, Frankenstein and Wolf-Features!'

'What do you mean?' asked Katie.

I unscrewed the top of my trusty half-bottle of vodka-flavoured paint stripper, and as their eyes went hungrily/thirstily to it I saw their glory days of graveyards, tattoos and suburban wildness, almost gone now, flash up in front of them, and I knew I'd won. I leaned in towards them conspiratorially. 'It's like this . . .'

11

It was weird going back up Clifton Hill, with the Dracules
giggling furtively in tow, towards the house I'd been in so
many times as a friend, this time as a wrecker. Except I
never really had been a friend, had I? Face it – people like
that don't actually make friends with people like me. They
might pretend to, so they can get something out of you,
but it's all make believe. And you know, you might think
it's a weird thing to say, 'So they can get something out of
you,' when they were so rich and famous and I was just a
poor little nobody – but that's the one thing rich people
can't buy; the experience of real life. And obviously that was
the thing they wanted, to 'inspire' them, if you can call it
that, for their effing nasty Chav Chic Collection.

As I turned the key that Duane had slipped me, I got
a first whiff of the way the house smelt – of ironing and
starch and a strong, strange, sort of sad perfume that I
knew was Guerlain's L'Heure Bleue. In the days when I'd
mistaken them for my friends, it had seemed to sum up
how exotic and special they were, but now I could only
smell the sharpness and the sourness beneath the powdery
flowers, and it made me catch my breath as I led the Dracules into the darkness of the hallway.

See, this is another thing. When we'd been 'friends' the
darkness of the house, all the draperies and black wood and
clutter, made me feel it was a sort of refuge from the mad,

loud, blaring, glaring world I was used to – the in-yer-face
starkness of being poor and trashy. But now I simply saw
it as further proof of how nasty they were – of how much
they had to hide. My mum's windows may have been a bit
dirty – well, filthy actually – but she never even bothered
to hang nets up because she's got NOTHING TO HIDE!
Apart from the fiddling of her bennies of course, that and
the stolen goods. But you know what I mean – nothing
BAD. Nothing sinister – like screwing underage kids, for
instance, or pretending to be someone's mate just so you
could go on to rip the piss out of them for pleasure and
profit. Little things like that.

'Whoah! They Goths then?' Josh exclaimed as I closed
the front door behind them.

'No, they've just got a lot to hide. That's why it's so
dark.' I stood there in the hallway, and I put my hands on
my hips, and I smiled in a big way; I felt like a conductor
of an orchestra in the moments before the music starts –
all the different elements of destruction that I was going to
encourage and pull together laid out in front of me. I
turned to the Dracules, who were staring at me expectantly.

'Well, let's start at the top, shall we?' An idea suddenly
occurred to me. 'Let's go and start where "the magic happens". Like in *Cribs*!'

We ran up the stairs and I led them into the master
bedroom, right where I'd found young Duane in the
naughty naked nude that fateful day. 'Here it is!' I whipped
out my trusty half-bottle of Vladivar and chucked it to
Katie, who I calculated to be the weakest link; she caught

it expertly and decanted a third of it down her neck in one gulp, then passed it on. Before I knew it I was staring at an empty, when an inspired thought struck me.

I pulled back the duvet to expose the spotless white sheet. 'That sheet's something called a Frette. Apparently it's got a thread count of nine hundred and sodding eighty. Which means that it cost an effing fortune.' I fished in my bag and threw an old flick-knife I'd nicked off Jesus on to the bed. 'Which means you get extra points for slashing it to buggery.' I looked on happily as they squabbled over the blade, then slipped downstairs looking for a refill.

They were still where I thought they'd be – a couple of the Bacardi Breezers Baggy and Aggy had always made sure they had in for me. At the time it had seemed really thoughtful, but now I saw it as it was – just another way to put me at my ease and get what they wanted out of me; inspiration for my humiliation. And of COURSE they had to get 'special' drinks in for me – of COURSE I couldn't drink simple, sophisticated white wine like they did. Of course I needed something the colour of sweeties, loaded with sugar, for my rubbishy tastes . . . talk about a spoonful of sugar helps the medicine go down! Well, it was THEY who were going to be taking their medicine now – and as I fished the brace of Breezers out of the cooler, I noted with pleasure that they were both watermelon – the livid red one. Revenge was going to be sweet, OK, sweeter than Sugar – and so COLOURFUL in places as well!

Upstairs, Katie and Josh were rediscovering their dark side with a vengeance – the mattress looked like a giant dead sheepdog, there was so much stuff spilling out of it. I pulled the top off a Breezer with my teeth and poured it all over what was left of the bed – it looked like some girl had had the world's worst period on it, which made me smile when I considered the snide way they talked about women. Then I drank the other one straight down.

'Oi!' squealed Katie. 'Share and share alike!'

'There's a sea of wine in the kitchen. And stickies and stuff on the drinks trolley in the living room,' I advised her. As she and Josh romped downstairs whooping, I had a further flash of inspiration and I called downstairs after them. 'And bring me up a bottle of Scotch – see if you can see one called The Macallan! Or anything that looks pricey!'

I went over to the long seat that opened up like a box, and found the red leather albums with all B&A's cuttings in, and I introduced my little friend blade-features to their glorious career – he seemed quite cut up about it! I was just finishing up when the Dracules bounced back into the room moaning about the expensive vodka they'd found in the kitchen. 'Grey Goose! – what sort of stupid name is that! Still, we DID find this black stuff! – good, innit!'

'Did you get the Scotch?' I asked somewhat sternly. It's weird – they were a good bit older than me, but they seemed so young and carefree. This was just a naughty romp to them, but to me it was deadly serious.

'Yeah, this Macallan, like you said!'

I took it and smiled; it made me happy to see there was at least half left, because I knew for a fact that the full bottle had cost more than a thousand pounds. I'd only seen my ex-friends sipping tiny amounts a couple of times – Aggy had confessed to me he hated the smell, but found it 'classier' than vodka, which could be seen as a 'girl's drink'. And we all know how stupid he thought girls were . . .

Hate the smell, did he? Well, he was going to have to get used to it, in his precious boudoir at least!

'You gonna drink it, Shugs? Never had you down as a Scotch girl –'

I unscrewed the cap as I walked towards the en suite. 'No, I'm not going to drink it, and neither are they . . . and that's going to get right – up – their – NOSES!'

They'd showed me how the steam cubicle worked, ages ago it seemed, when I was still a bright-eyed little girl oohing and ahhing over the Wonder Of Them and their palace of fun – me being the fun in question, as it turned out. So it was no problem knowing where the essential oils were meant to go. Lavender for tranquility, peppermint for get-up-and-go – and a really expensive Scotch, almost half a bottleful, for feeling sick as an effing dog for an extremely long time when you woke up in the morning to face another day of creativity and crushing people's dreams . . .

I poured it all in and turned it up full.

The Dracules rocked up behind me. 'Whoa! – DRY ICE!' Then, 'IT STINKS!'

'Not half as bad as it's going to.' I turned to look at them. 'Right – you've drunk enough of that black vodka – the rest goes over the bedroom carpet.' Thick and white as snow on Aspen, natch! 'Thassit! Now go and open that Grey Goose – you deserve it.'

I wanted to be alone to create my masterpiece, didn't I? I looked around the lovely bathroom, where once I could happily have lived. Gagging from the smell of Scotch, I smashed the little telly on the stalk and stuck the business end of an ornamental cut-throat razor through the stereo speakers. Garish lotions and potions galore made a lovely swirly sight on the snow-leopard-print carpet, and to my surprise I was so into my task that I pulled off the leopard-print toilet seat with my bare hands.

Katie put her head round the door as I was doing it. 'Gosh, Maria! – I mean, FUCK! You must really hate these people –'

I felt embarrassed being caught in the act – it seemed like it should be private to hate someone that much. I spoke to her without turning round.

'Get Josh and go and smash up the guest rooms – there's three of them. Then meet me downstairs by the drinks trolley and we'll finish off.'

It was mostly done anyway, but it's those finishing touches that make all the difference, I find. So I carefully shredded the shower curtain with its lovely print of techni-colour dolphins – and doing so I recalled how much I'd admired it once, only to be amazed when B&A fell about screeching with laughter: 'Oh bless her! Shugs, it's not MEANT to be "lovely"! – it's meant to be KITSCH!' I hadn't really understood what kitsch was at the time, and I didn't want to ask and look DUMB in front of my FRIENDS, so I'd just smiled sweetly with them. But as my little friend dutifully did his job, I knew all at once

TOTALLY what kitsch was – it was just yet another way to feel superior to other people because they had less money than you. Boy, talk about the scenic route!

Well, it didn't look lovely OR kitsch now, I reflected as I stepped away. Task complete, I started going through their vast wicker baskets of smellies, making sure I rescued enough Bvlgari soaps to sort me out for the next three Christmases, when I came across, at the bottom of one, just about the BIGGEST bottle of L'Heure Bleue you ever did see; not a spray either, just a great big bottle with a stopper, like some showpiece from a posh chemist. I laughed, grabbed it and ran down the stairs two at a time.

The Dracules were feeling no pain by now, having bravely overcome their aversion to quality vodka and consumed the best part of a bottle of Grey Goose. I scowled at them – this was a serious mission we were on here and they were acting like it was Living-Dead Night at Hector's House, cocktails 2–4–1! 'Did you do the other bedrooms, like I said?'

Josh nodded, then hiccuped. 'Sweet, Sugar!'

'Then get cooking.' I flung open the vast American fridge, where once I used to stand for minutes at a time watching in childlike fascination as the ice-making machine did its mysterious, magical thing. What a fucking innocent IDIOT I'd been!

'Milk on the carpets, prawns down the back of all the sofas and soft chairs. We'll do a right Jamie Oliver!' I opened their retro-trash cupboard and took out an armful of the pristine, unopened boxes of American cookies they'd practically wet themselves cooing over. 'And then you can take a break. Only one biscuit from each box, mind you. And then chuck the rest on to the milk and stomp 'em well in. No slacking!'

I opened a few more drawers – ah, their Cybercandy stash! Cybercandy is like this amazing little sweet shop down in the North Laines where you can buy all sorts of softies and sweets and chocolate from all around the world, especially Japan and America. The only drawback is the prices – £4.80 for a Vodka Lix lollipop! I'd have to work close-on an hour just to earn the price of one of them – still, I reflected, as I poked around among the Skittles Littles, Mike and Ikes and Tart 'n' Tinys, that was nothing that a five-fingered discount couldn't take care of.

I called to the Dracules, who were stamping biscuits into the milky carpets with lip-biting concentration. 'Get over here when you've finished and fill your boots. Look! – Snake Venom lollies, these could have been made for you two weirdies! Then you can bail – I've got private stuff to do. Personal. Cheers!'

I left them exclaiming over the Cybercandy drawer and broke open a very decent bottle of Bolly from the fridge. I needed to be alone for the next bit – and I needed it to be a celebration, hence the bubbly. A solitary celebration. I went into the workroom and closed the door behind me. I locked it. Then I poured Bolly all over the blade. To make it pure for the task that lay ahead.

Which was the not inconsiderable one of taking back my honour – an honour which I had, let's be fair, spent the best part of seventeen years pissing away. But choosing to fritter a thing away is a far different thing to having it snatched from you – it's the difference between having power and being powerless, which is just about the biggest difference in the world so far as I can tell.

And there, in front of me, was the skilfully-honed proof of the biggest and most professional shafting I'd ever had the pleasure of, worn by a docile row of dummies with their blank faces neatly labelled.

And the names of my dishonour were (as already established by the meeting with young Trulocke in Macky D's):

WHITE-TRASH TINKERBELL
PRAM-FACED PRICKTEASE
LATE AGAIN!
PIKEY PRINCESS
CHIPSHOP CHIC

and not forgetting

MUM'S ABORTION

And as I stood there facing them, it was like looking at every dummy who'd ever disrespected me, all of them. I don't know exactly what happened next – it was a bit of a blur.

And when I came round and was conscious again, the dummies were dressed in rags, just ribbons of cloth hanging off them. And the silver velvet chaise longue from

Rume was slashed to ribbons too. And the big bottle of L'Heure Bleue was smashed all over it and the sour, sad smell beneath the first shimmer of the scent seemed to sum up my whole experience in that house.

I went into the downstairs toilet and I took out my special Stila 'Sugar' lipstick that Aggy had given me and I couldn't help it, I wrote 1 OF YR YOUNG FRENDZ WUZ ERE! on the mirror. It was cheeky but not daft, I thought – it told them it was me, but also that I knew about Duane and that it wouldn't be clever to go to the police. In fact I was congratulating myself so wholeheartedly on the way out that it wasn't till I was halfway down Clifton Hill that I realized that not only had I wanted them to KNOW I was there – but even weirder, that I hadn't even robbed anything! (Just soaps, like you would in a hotel, so it don't count.)

What did the two things mean together, I wondered? By the time I got to the bottom of the hill, I thought I might have worked it out –

It must have been love!

12

Talking of which, what was it with Asif? Was it love, was it lust, was it killing time till something came along which I wouldn't feel the need to ask myself questions about? Whatever, it felt nice – it had the relaxed quality of an old relationship and the excitement of a new one. In fact, all it lacked was plain, simple MAGIC.

Asif was beautiful – more beautiful than Kim. He was also, if you want to get smutty about it, better equipped sex-wise – I mean, she had those tiny little hands, like a kiddy's! But I don't know – I didn't get that kick-in-the-stomach thing from him. Don't get me wrong; if anyone's going to be kicking someone in the stomach, or anywhere for that matter, it's generally going to be yours truly. But in my experience, it IS a tremendous thrill, in a weird kind of way, when finally you're NOT in control, when you're used to being the one on top.

For instance, I knew that Kimmy was nowhere near as tough as me – the way she used to look UP to me was actually quite sad – but there was something about her that made me so horny I actually felt helpless. Even watching the uptight little cow test the smoke alarms at Sweet Towers, holding the chair steady and looking up her skirt – the nearest I'D ever get, or the only reason I'd ever WANT to put anyone on a pedestal, ha ha! – made me feel weak with longing sometimes. It was like the physical pain you get from laughing hard at school, that agonizing ecstasy that just goes when you grow up. This is going to sound well mental, but perhaps the reason we're all so desperate to fall in love is BECAUSE, not in spite of, the fact that it makes us feel helpless again, like being a little kid – and if you're having to be tough all the time, well, that's some sort of freedom.

I'd felt like a kid a lot of the time when I was with Kim – you could say, 'Yeah, Shugs, but you WERE only fifteen!' – but believe me, if you knew me better then you'd know that I hadn't been a child since I was twelve. Yet somehow with her I got it back – even though we were meant to have 'corrupted' each other or something, which was why her parents whisked her away like that. It was like sex with her wiped out all the too-much-too-young stuff.

I didn't feel like a kid with Asif though. I felt that every time I had sex with him, I absorbed a bit of all that terrible stuff he'd been through. Kim had had an easy life, and it rubbed off on me; Asif had had a rotten time, and so did that. And I had enough baggage of my own to cart around, let's face it, without prancing up to all and sundry and squealing, 'Hi! My name is Maria and I will be your bag carrier for the night!'

That was the theory – the practice, though, was Those Eyes and That Mouth, and they'd do until plain old Magic came along again. So I shared his pain and my sandwiches, and sang his hymns, and rubbed his back when he'd start crying about what his lot had to put up with in Pakistan. We were in it together, the way I looked at it, and we might as well do our best to help each other through, especially sex-wise. The way I see it, and the way Asif might have put it if he'd been a dirty-minded blasphemer, horizontal is the good Lord's apology for vertical.

Nevertheless, as I waited in the rain for the bus to Stanwick that night, I was starting to regret my decision to kick the horsey habit. Facing another eight hours of wasting my brains and beauty in that place without actually *being* wasted didn't seem a whole lot of fun. For about a minute after redecorating Ag and Bag's place, I'd been buzzing with what I'd taken to have been a natural high – but, as with every high, natural or chemical, you've gotta pay for it with the comedown, and mine had kicked in without so much as an eighth to ease the pain.

I'd got my revenge on the paedo pair – but where did that leave me exactly? I wasn't going to get my chance any time soon to make the pages of the *Argus* as high-fashion's latest must-have muse, that was for sure! I'd tried not to get too carried away with the whole idea – I knew I wasn't about to be strutting my stuff down the catwalks of London, Paris or Milan any time soon – but I did at least think there was a chance I'd maybe see some chick strutting through the North Laines next summer looking well sweet in one of the designs I'd inspired. Kizza once told me she thought I was terrified of being as ordinary and boring as everyone else; at the time I'd had to shut the daft dyke up by sticking my tongue down her throat, but of course she was right – I'm terrified of being ordinary.

I'm not scared of spiders and I'm not scared of snakes – hardly, with my track record! – but when I'm walking home at night and I peer in the lighted windows at the happy little families living their happy little lives, I feel a sense of absolute panic, like you're meant to feel if you're standing on the ledge of a skyscraper with no safety net – vertigo, that's it. I know that some people look into other people's rooms and wish it was them – but being a wife, having a family, I just don't get it. It's like being dead – only you have to do housework!

Would be different if I got Ren back, though . . . my little Ren. Just me and her.

And Asif. And possibly Kimmy. And Dr Fox too, if I could swing it with Asif and Kimmy.

I shook myself. What a perve I was! And come to think of it, what right did I have to sneer at other people! They were ordinary inside their little boxes, all tucked up tight – I was ordinary outside of the respectable loop. And for me, ordinary meant cleaning bogs and watching other people fly off to places I was only ever likely to see on *Holiday Reps*. Talking of which, on *Holiday Showdown* a while back there was this family from Bristol who'd only ever been to one place for their holidays – Bristol. Just like my mum and Brighton! Roots, who'd have 'em! – roots are OK for trees but crap for people; just another way of holding you back and keeping you down and spoiling your fun. Roots are like an umbilical cord round your neck all your life. Roots suck!

For a few weeks I'd caught a glimpse of a different life

– a life where, following the runaway runway success of the Sugar-coated collection, my proud and grateful new friends had tucked me neatly and firmly under their privileged wing and carried me into a shiny new future. But however much the motherfrockers might have claimed that the merest glimpse of a naked chick made them want to vom, like most men they just couldn't resist screwing one. Then – again just like most men – they'd dropped me right back where they found me. Which was standing in the cold, looking forward to another night picking chewing gum off tables and emptying ashtrays. Seemed such a waste of brains and body, if you ask me – which of course no one ever did. So I was, quite justifiably, in a raging mood when I stepped off the bus, but the sight of Asif waiting for me with a look of concern and a big flowery umbrella made me feel a little better. And giving him a quick feel made me feel better still.

He squirmed and sniggered as I groped him. 'I didn't want you to get wet,' he said as he shoved the umbrella into my hand. His voice was all soft and concerned as he put his arm round me and we headed towards the airport.

'That makes a change!' I nudged him.

He laughed. 'There's – what you're saying? – method in my mania!'

'Madness, you mean!' You couldn't but laugh at his pretty ways. AND he smelt of curry. I'm not saying that in a bad way – I totally heart curry. So that cheered me up too.

'Because if you get wet,' he went on, 'you might get a

cold. And if you get a cold –' and now a deliciously lustful light danced in his eyes – 'I won't be able to do this . . .' He pulled me up against him so I could feel just how pleased he was to see me; put it this way, it reminded me of when I was little and Suzy used to to put her arms as far apart as she could and go 'I-LOVE-YOU-THIS-MUCH!' in a slightly too intense way that used to make me scream like a girl and run off and hide in the dog's basket.

Not that I was going to run and hide this time! He gave me a long slow kiss, and looking up into his beautiful face I decided tonight might not be so bad after all. 'Fancy a quickie in the supply cupboard later?' I grinned and ran my hand over his bum as we dumped our coats and headed for the staffroom. But then I heard Kathleen's voice come whining through the walls like Black & Decker's finest, straight through my skull, and I realized I'd cheered up too soon. Ever since the rosary-munching drudge had clocked that there was something cooking between me and Asif, she'd done her worst to make sure we couldn't get our paws on each other during working hours; he'd be banished to buff the floors in check-in and I'd be at the other end of the airport on loo duty. The glamorous life!

13

Sure enough I spent the next few hours as the Cif-spraying sidekick of the deranged old dwarf, listening to her rant on about how much of a burden it was being the *only one who ever cleaned anything properly round here*, and how the rest of them (meaning Kathryn, wild guess) never even did a half-decent job – I guess they'd forgotten to iron the bog roll, lick the urinals clean with their own tongues or something equally satanic. Course there was nothing the twisted troll loved more than finding a bin that hadn't been emptied or a desk that had gone undusted; she became so excited by any evidence that everyone except her was total pants at their paid employment that she practically wet herself on the spot.

I knew my routine off by heart by now; I did a bit of 'innit!' and threw in a few 'lazy bastards!' out of the goodness of my heart – my mum's a Catholic and, believe me, I know how these broads get a rush from playing the hard-done-by martyr, all they need's the audience to make it complete – but after a bit I'd had enough and let her rant off down to check-in while I flopped down on a seat and lit a fag. I sat there in a blue funk, smoking and watching holidaymakers till it was time for my break, when I dragged myself back to the staffroom.

Kathleen looked up and gave me evils with knobs on

as I threw myself over Asif. As if she'd say no if the Pope put her on a promise!

'And where exactly did you disappear to, Maria! You can't just go wandering off whenever you feel like it, you know – this airport isn't going to clean itself! I had to do check-in all on my own – it's a wonder I managed to get it done in time, though with my poor back giving me jip all the while it's not something I can say I enjoyed, thank you very much!'

Yeah, right – the old bag loved it! In fact she'd probably be happier if I skedaddled every night and left her to get on with it, she's that into the feeling-good-feeling-bad shtick. Still, I couldn't be arsed to argue, so I mumbled something about a kid projectile vomiting and diarrhoeaing – both ends burning! – in Arrivals. And I swear the mad cow looked jealous! – clearly she was well teed off that I might have stolen yet another tasty job from right under her nose, because after break she let me off the leash and sent me to clear up in the departure lounge while she hot-footed it over to Arrivals to see if any tiny speck of sick had survived to suffer her tender ministrations. Freak!

At this time of night, Departures was usually rammed with 18–30s catching late flights to the party destinations of the world – and these happy holidaymakers had no intention of waiting till the plane touched down – or indeed, till it took off – to get the party started. Their final destination was alcoholic oblivion – and these were already well on the way to needing the brown paper bag in the seat pocket in front of them. The bar was full of hard-bodied girls and beer-bellied boys (ooh, there's my inner lezzer raising its ugly head again! – OK, some of the boys were passing fit) knocking back the booze and already mistaking the fluorescent lighting of the airport for the shameless, blameless blaze of some sun-soaked, sin-soaked island; looking at them, I instantly recognized my people – the similarly shameless, blameless English youth, taking their leisure and pleasure with a savage innocence. I felt an almost painful pull towards them, and an equal revulsion towards the work world I was currently billeted in.

Something in me snapped, and at the same time something *pinged!* back into place. I might have been watching the party from the wrong side of the rope, but what was to stop me from ducking under it and joining in for a while?

A group of girls were shrieking and laughing and shouting over each other by the bar; they were wearing identical gear – cropped baby-pink Ts with FALLEN ANGEL scrawled across their tits in sparkling silver scrawl, tiny denim hot pants and cowboy boots. It was clear that this ensemble had been chosen by the size tens of the pack, cos when I say 'identical' the same outfit couldn't have looked more different. Every size and shape of chick was either slipped into the clobber like it was a second skin or wedged into it like a hippo in a condom. A classic blonde Barbie Girl, all big tits, tiny waist and long baby-Bambi legs was leaning against the bar with one St Tropezed arm slung round a dark-eyed Natalie Portman looky-likey who was wearing a veil and a LEARNER plate. I'd bet my miserable week's wages that Barbie had been in charge of picking out the outfits – not that I blamed her for show-casing her wares so wantonly. I'd once worn a skirt out to Creation that was so short some sarky student said to me, 'That's a nice belt – why don't you get some more material like it and make a skirt as well!'

Barbie Girl grabbed a tequila shot and a slice of lemon from a long line that were on the bar ready to go. 'Shut up and get drinking,' she shouted. 'To Vic – the poor cow! I had him before she did, and let's say I'm glad I only did him for the practice, because he was no damn use for any-thing else!'

Vic started to object – 'Sazza! You bitch! – but was drowned out by the chorus of "TO VIC!" followed by squeals of delight as they knocked back the shots.

'Right, next one!' commanded Blondie.

The girls were being perved at by a bunch of lads that by the look of their well-stacked shoulders and broken noses might well have been a rugby team. I don't usually go for rugby players – most of them seem to be posh twats who think you're not worth talking to if you didn't 'school' with the royals but yet still think it's OK to grope your arse without asking. I mean, working-class boys are meant to be rough – but at least they've got an excuse. When someone's had a fortune spent on their education though, isn't it a bit weird that they communicate in grunts and lunges?

But there was one of this lot I wouldn't have minded getting in a scrum with. He was leaning against the bar lazily scratching his mid-section – an improvement on the Neanderthal nut-gathering I was used to, I suppose – lifting his T-shirt (which read GO HOME, YOUR VILLAGE IS MISSING ITS IDIOT: pot, kettle, wack!) to reveal not just a tantalizing glimpse of his Calvin Klein crackers but also a taut, toned stomach that made Gavin Henson look like he was letting himself go a bit. He was a flesh-and-bone cliché – tall, dark and doable – and better still while the rest of his teammates were drooling over the Fallen Angels he'd clocked my appreciative stare and was helping himself to a large serving of perving as he ran his eyes all over me like a bad case of carpet burn. Workers' playtime!

Yeah, yeah – I hadn't forgotten about my big-eyed buddy with the magical expanding umbrella. But what Asif didn't see wasn't going to upset him and it wasn't like I was planning to actually DO anything. I just fancied having a little fun before I forgot what it was, is all.

So I had only just decided to let Hooray Hottie buy me a drink when I realized that Barbie Girl was thinking along similar lines; she flicked back her hair, downed her tequila, winked at her mates and shimmied over to my prey. Well, I wasn't about to let a little competition spoil my night, so checking that the poppers on my uniform – btw, NEVER underestimate the power of a uniform as boy-bait – had given up their futile attempts to keep my puppies under control, I unholstered my Mr Muscle and strutted into battle.

Barbie Girl was teetering towards him, rolling her hips, batting her lashes and sticking out her tits so far I was surprised she hadn't fallen over. I *gently* nudged her out of the way and took aim at my target totty. 'Sorry to barge in, but it's my job to keep things clean, see, and I was wondering if you had . . . ah . . . anything that needs polishing? Anything I could give a good rub?' I let a slow grin slide across my face as I looked up at him and winked in slo-mo; OK, it wasn't subtle, but it's girl-meets-boy-meat we're talking about here, not world peace.

He gave me a big cheeky grin – gentlemen prefer blondes, my arse they do! – and leaned towards me, giving himself a good view down my carefully customized tunic. 'Mmm . . . I can only see one thing round here that might be a bit dirty.'

He looked up from my cleavage and we stared at each other for a couple of seconds, eyes sparkling, before we both cracked up laughing.

'Maria Sweet – you can call me Sugar.'

'Sweet to meet you, Sugar. I'm Cameron, but you can call me Cam. Or any time!'

I groaned and stuck out my tongue.

'Can I get you a drink – or are you going to get me one? That's your job, after all, isn't it . . . keeping the punters happy no matter what the cost . . .'

I kicked him playfully and he yelped.

'Oi, Cam,' a voice boomed in our direction, rudely interrupting our romp. 'You can't have 'em both, mate – that's just greedy. Share the wealth! 'Less of course you want to film a bit of girl-on-girl on your phone and show us all later . . .'

That was when I realized that Barbie Girl was still standing behind me looking quite like she wanted to rip my eyes out and play ping-pong with 'em. I had a choice – I could come out with a poisonous put-down and completely annihilate her, or I could show mercy, save her from total humiliation and get girl-points. Nothing looks less attractive than competing over a man – about as sexy as squabbling about the last seat on a bus; like there won't be another along in a minute! So more through vanity than virtue, I played nice.

"Ey, Barbie, what you drinking – something pink, I bet! Cam's buyin', so put your order in. And your mate about to go to the slaughter – sorry, altar. Love the T, by the way!'

She looked at me coldly for a moment like she was about to open fire, but then she seemed to decide like it wasn't worth it – sooo the right decision! – and gave me a wary smile. 'Cheers – it's for my mate's hen do. We've all got one, see?' She gestured in the direction of her friends.

'Hey – you lot!' I shouted over to them. 'These kiddies are buying us all a drink. Get in there!' Then I turned and flashed the lads my best I-Bet-It's-Not-Butter-wouldn't-melt smile and sat back to enjoy the party.

An hour later and at least three hens had flown the coop, copping off in various dark corners with Cam's lot while the rest of us shared bottles of Smirnoff Ice and our life stories. 'So Vic's the first one of us to get hitched,' Barbie-Saz was telling me, all teary-eyed as she ruffled the bride-to-be's hair, 'but we've warned her that she's definitely not allowed to turn into one of those boring bitches who's never allowed off her leash to party with the girls. Like that saddo she's marrying shows every sign of wanting her to.'

'Do one!' Vic advised her friend enthusiastically. 'Like that's ever gonna happen. No freakin' way!' Then her eyes went all soft and her voice all soppy. Sort of like a Bratz doll having the abdabs. 'But he's soooo lovely, isn't he, Saz? He is, Sugar – he's lovely, not just fit, he's really sweet and funny too.'

'You make him sound like one of those effing ice lollies with a joke inside!' shrieked Saz, finding herself hilarious and not without reason, I thought.

Vic shoved her. Clearly their relationship was based on shoving and sarcasm more than sugar and spice, and it made me think of me and Kim for a moment. I looked at Vic and Saz and I wondered if they'd ever snogged each other after a few WKD Blues too many, but if they had, it was long gone now as Vic continued bigging up her intended.

'He's so cool, you'd have to see him to believe him, Sugar – hey, you should come to the wedding! – shouldn't she come to the wedding, Saz!'

'Yeah, you should – as good an excuse to get trashed as any!' She looked as if she was about to start welling up again – all very moving, but it was starting to get a bit wet and windy for me; we were meant to be having FUN, for fuck's sake!

'Cheers, chix, but wedding cake makes me feel like heaving – been there and done that before I can vote, and it didn't exactly end happy ever after. Or even for six months, come to that!' I snorted with disgust, thinking about Mark and Ren and the whole mess of it. Then I caught the look of alarm on Vic's face and felt bad about raining on her poor misguided parade. 'I mean, I'm sure you'll have a lovely marriage and that, but all I'm saying is that it wasn't like that for me. Here, pass us that.' I took a massive swig of Ice, drew a deep breath and then embarked on the edited highlights of the whole sorry saga. When I was done with my tale of woe the girls were momentarily mute with outrage. Then the slagging started!

'Bastard!' spat Saz, giving my shoulder a sympathetic squeeze.

'Yeah, what a cold fucker!' chorused the other Fallen Angels.

'Yeah, fucking bastards, they're all the bleeding same!' shouted over one of the boys, and then we were back where I wanted us to be, falling and fooling around, laughing out loud at all the crap life kept throwing at you – always and forever, till death us do part – downing our drinks and not giving a damn about anything except right here, right now.

'Could the last remaining passengers for flight BA1036 to Ibiza PLEASE make their way to GATE SIX IMME-DIATELY, where your plane is READY TO DEPART.' Even though she said please, it was clear the tannoy voice meant, 'The fucking idiots who are meant to be on flight BA1036 better get their friggin' arses to gate six in the next fucking second or I'm going to make those drunken wasters regret it very bitterly indeed . . .'

'Screw it!' screeched Saz in my ear, spitting Smirnoff Ice down my neck. 'That's our sodding flight – MOVE!'

My blissed-out voddy daze was interrupted by body after body, girls and guys, grabbing me in clumsy hugs and/or planting smackers on my face and swearing they'd call me when they got back and/or see me at the wedding. Then in a hustle of muscle and/or a posse of pink my new friends were gone, clattering their eager way to the departure gate and all points pleasure-bound.

I stood there feeling miserable and/or manky, half-pissed in my polyester uniform, the skivvy who didn't get to go to the ball after all because her fairy godmother had probably just got on an easyJet to Alicante. Staring out of the huge window on to the runway, I watched as plane after plane took off, the twinkling lights leading the way to some warm and wicked paradise island where the Slow Comfortable Screws never stopped – while all I had to look forward to was a bollocking from Kathleen and a cold, wet trudge back to ASBO Towers.

For a minute I almost wished I was back inside – no work, three meals a day and drugs on tap. The good old days! But my brief pity party was suddenly gatecrashed by a pair of silky dark arms snaking round my neck and a voice so sincere it could strip both your teeth of their enamel and, if you were the soppy sort, your body of its kit in about five seconds flat.

'You know,' Asif whispered. 'I know what you are thinking when you watch the planes. And sometimes England seems cold to me too. And it isn't even my home, as it is yours. But just because the sun shines in a country doesn't mean happiness can be found there, as my people know.'

'And that was a broadcast of behalf of the Christians of Pakistan,' I said tetchily, knowing I was being a bitch and not being able to help it. Come on, the way I did it, how long and how thoroughly, being a bitch was practically my religion by now!

I felt him edge away from me, and I was sorry I'd added yet another injury to those he'd already suffered, and him so young and sweet. Still, he wasn't giving up.

'All I meant to say was that there is more to freedom than the sun shining, and more to sadness than the rain falling. It's cold here yet you have warmth, with your family, as I do with mine.' He turned me round to face him; I couldn't meet his eyes. (So I stared at his crotch instead, to cheer me up.) 'And I can honestly say, Sugar, even though I don't speak English so good, that there really is nowhere in the world I'd rather be right now than here with you.'

If I hadn't swallowed the entire contents of the Smirnoff Ice bottle in my hand, I'd have spewed it all over him. 'Bloody hell, Asif! Where the freak d'you learn a line like that?!'

With this he looked so sad even I decided that it was time to clock off bitch-duty for the day. I'd had my fun and I'd have more. For now, I had my boy. He'd seen enough nastiness to last him a lifetime – and I never did like following the herd.

I pulled him close. 'You speak English great. Better than me and I was born here. Come on – let's see what else you do good.' And as I helped myself to one of his trademark long kisses – patent pending, probably, they were that good – I couldn't help thinking that maybe Brighton in the rain wasn't so bad after all.

14

Well, if Shugs couldn't go to the ball – the rave in Ibiza, rather – then the ball would have to come to Shugs. Face it, there were worse places to be than Brighton, whatever the weather, and I had my love to keep me warm. Well, my teenage lust.

So I decided to give young Asif Sugar's Sensational Shagtastic Seaside Tour of Brighton. Like I said, Susie used to drive me mad saying there was no point in going away on holiday when you live in a holiday town, but now I had to admit, maybe she had a point. Let's not delude ourselves here – if I could choose between caipirinhas at the Café del Mar or coffee at the Western Road Starbucks, I'd be blissed out on that beach before you can say bikini wax. But that was the whole sodding point, wunnit? – I didn't *have* that choice so I might as well make the most of what I did have. Which was a home-town that was always whoring itself to rich Londoners any chance it got, but which I still had a soft spot for, and a big-eyed boy to share it with. Sweet.

Organized tours of this place are usually one of two things – totally straight, like the Pavilion and stuff, or totally twisted. Like on the main bus tour, right, there's no warning or anything; one minute this posh bird's voice is coming through this speaker banging on about that fat royal git that had the Pav built for his married piece or something, and the next minute she's going into all the gory details about this dude, Tony Mancini, that killed this girl and cut her up and stuffed her in a trunk! I had to talk nineteen to the dozen to keep She-Ra and Evil-Lyn from hearing that stuff when we went on it one day – one of Mum's cost-cutting day trips – though to be fair it does come in useful whenever I want to make 'em do something they're not keen on. Like, 'Go on, Evil, nip down the shop for me, or Tony Mancini'll come tonight when you're asleep and cut you up into little bits and stuff you into my new pink Topshop handbag!' It's good for people to know their local history, so I'm doing good by doing good, as it were.

'So. What's your favourite things?' I asked Asif when we were changing to go home.

He smiled at me, all soppy like. 'You. My faith. Though not necessarily in that order . . .'

'Oi!' I thumped him. 'Try getting your Bible to give you a blow job!'

He laughed and caught me by the wrists. I've noticed that about proper religious people; they can laugh about their God-bothering, they don't want to cut your head or hands off like the Muslims always seem to want to. 'Why are you so interested in my favourite things, anyway?'

'Wanna take you out, don't I? On your own unique Shugs-shaped tour. Not the usual tourist stuff and not just a bar-crawl like the hens and slags.' I laughed appreciatively here, nudging Asif sharply when he didn't immediately do so as well.

He gave a few swift sniggers in self-defence, then

thought about what I'd said. 'Well . . . I should like to go to a museum. I have never been to English museum, and everybody talks about them.'

'Hmm . . .' I eyed him suspiciously. 'I'll take your word for it.' What a bunch of sad bastards he must hang out with!

'So, we could start with a museum . . . ?'

'And amp it up from there? – OK!' Face it, if we started with a museum, it could only get better, coun'it!

But which museum? There was the main one down by the Old Steine but I'd been dragged round that one so many times by school that the thought made me want to heave, frankly – even the cute smiling giant pottery cat by the entrance, who purred and said stuff like MMM . . . PUT SOME MONEY IN THE KITTY when you fed him a few coins couldn't lure me there. Another museum, think, think . . . I laughed at myself racking my brains over one, cos of course if it had been a crack dealer or an after-hours hooch-den, I'd have had a dozen right on speed dial. Museums, though, that was a different kettle of endangered cod.

'Look, meet me tomorrow morning at ten, the sea end of Ship Street, and we'll take it from there. And come prepared!' I jumped up, slapped his bum and gathered my things together.

'You mean with umbrella?'

'No, with condoms, of course!'

Even on a breezy winter's day Brighton seafront sparkled in the sun, and as I leaned against the seafront railings having a quick fag and waiting for Asif to creep in from Crawley, I thought that despite all the crap that had happened to me in my home-town, there was just something magical about it that kept you coming back for more, or in my case never getting around to leaving in the first place. When I was little I used to think that that old hymn actually said 'All things *Brighton* beautiful', and even though I'd felt a right teat when I found out what it really was, the words still rang in my mind whenever I went to the seafront on a sunny day. That old saying 'Hope springs eternal', which we used to snigger at at school cos it had 'breast' in the rest of it could have been written about Brighton – it may have been the accidental OD capital of Britain, but no way could it ever have won in the suicide stakes. There was just something about this place, no matter what the weather was like, which made you feel that life was worth living.

Brighton's notorious as the place that Londoners come to for uni, or a dirty weekend, or a club night, and never go home from again. And if it looked that good to Londoners, how must it look to Asif, after the heat and dust and hatred of Islamabad?

I was trying to get my head around seeing it from his point of view when he came up behind me and said in my ear, 'ip for them . . .'

'Don't be kinky,' I cackled. 'And anyway, you couldn't afford 'em.' I took his hand and dragged him across the road to the pier. I needed some decent thrills inside me before I braved a museum.

We went to the gypsy caravan, where a man with the

bluest eyes and the fastest talking and the greatest name –
Ivor Fireman! – told our fortunes; we did the temporary
henna-tattoo shop, which, to be blunt, makes it look like
someone's scrawled on your arm with excrement – ASIF on
my arm, SUGER on his – and didn't see the misspelling
till it was too late. Then we ate crêpes and waffles all the
way up to the far end, where we went on the Super Booster.
We were lifted to thirty-eight metres with only the sea
beneath us and then dropped, going all the way from nothing to sixty miles an hour in less than three seconds!
Unfortunately, so did all those crêpes and waffles and that
Knickerbocker Glory Asif had put away.

'Respect! – I've never seen spewing quite like that,' I
complimented him as I wiped the sick from his chin.

'Never again!' he moaned. 'My stomach is still up there
somewhere, I feel!'

'You need a drink,' I decided – Sexy Nurse Sugar! – and
before he could register what I was doing I was pulling him
through the door of Horatio's Bar and lining up the Aftershocks.

Looking back, this was where it started, in the somewhat shabby, though convivial, surroundings of Horatio's
karaoke bar – the feeling that I was being watched; para-
doxically, by someone who wasn't there. That is, one Kim
Lewis, late of this parish, disappeared thief of my heart.
(Ish.) And I know that this makes me sound like some sort
of screaming nutter but it felt like that – like in the film
where the kid can see dead people. Course Kim wasn't
hiding under my bed and vomiting up poison, fingers

crossed, and she wasn't dead neither, hopefully, just packed off out of my evil reach. But maybe just like the girl in the film she was trying to give me a message – only in her case, the message was more of an accusation.

I swear, as I stood there at the bar, smiling at my boy who sat expectantly in a sea-view booth smiling right back at me, I could actually hear Kizza's voice, all high-pitched and high-horse like it went when she was about to start blubbing about some imagined slight or other. 'How could you take him to the pier, Maria? It was one of our special places! It was where I fell in with you! Surely even to you that's got to mean something!' . . . and on, and on, and on.

'Well, we never went on the Super Booster and spewed up our rings, cos it's only been there since 2006, so swivel!' I muttered under my breath as I carried the Aftershocks over to Asif.

But she just wouldn't quit. And the more the ghost of Kiz followed me around the pier, the more pissed off I started to get. Partly because no matter how sweet and sexy Asif was, everything we did felt sort of faded, finished before it was over – we were like a xerox of a xerox, and she was like my missing limb that still had a pain in it. But also, I couldn't believe her nerve. The hypocrisy!

OK, so I might not have been dead keen on doing that whole three-legged race 'couple' thing with Kim – or with anyone, come to that, it wasn't nothing personal! And if you wanna get picky about it, I s'pose me getting married and having a baby might have given her the impression I didn't want to live lezzily ever after with her, but still, if she'd been that into me she could at least have bothered to write me the odd letter when I was banged up. For all she knew some big scary dyke-features could have turned me into her own personal PlayStation and I could have been crying into my pillow every night waiting for just one SWALK from her to put everything right.

Course, as it turned out, it only took ten minutes till I owned the place and had all the big scary dyke-featureses within those walls running round waiting on me simply for the pleasure of it – natch – but the point I'm trying to make is that she didn't KNOW that and, clearly, she couldn't be arsed to find out. It's like I always used to say to her when we argued: why should I give her one hundred per cent when it was so obvious that she was gonna go to university, spend her freakin' 'gap year' travelling, graduate, travel again, meet a rich lesbian and live abroad – New York probably, a penthouse with a view of the Statue of Liberty. Whereas the furthest I was going, obviously, was the end of the pier.

OK, so as far as she knew I was still playing happy families, but it wouldn't have *hurt* her, I mean it wouldn't exactly have *drawn blood* for her to make sure, just on the off-chance I might be back on the meat market. And I realize I keep using the words 'knew', 'know' and that about her, but that's the point in a way, and that's why doing fun stuff with Asif wasn't coming up to how it used to be with Kim. Because, at the end of the day, she *knew* me, from the outside in, from my head to my toes – and she still loved me. Whereas Asif, frankly, ain't got a clue; I mean, I know he thinks I'm sexy and 'naughty' and whatever, not exactly the girl next door to the Pakistani Christian church – but that's not the half of it, is it! I mean, try hot girl-on-girl action, aggravated assault, teenage divorce and as yet unde-tected criminal damage – for starters. What I'm saying is – if he didn't know my previous, how could he know me? And if he didn't know me, how could he really love me?

It's not that I was nostalgic about me and Kim – I'm close enough to the scene of the sex-crime to remember that a lot of the time she irritated the hell out of me. And I've never been the sort of person to get all gooey eyed about the past – once you've done something, or someone for the last time, it's done – stick a fork in me, see ya anon, move on and keep moving. I mean, I'm so hot on closure I don't even use revolving doors if I can help it. Which was *exactly* why I was now so teed off about being stalked by the Ghost Of Kizza Past. Well, if she really wanted a front-row seat to see what I was up to in her absence, I'd give her a show to remember!

I sat there sipping my Aftershock, looking at the sea without seeing it, thinking Kim's favourite place/Asif's tour/Sugar's shag and how I could kill three birds with one stone, when suddenly it came to me. It was the 'three birds' idea that sparked it off, too!

The Booth Museum of Natural History! – yeah, I know, the excitement'll give us an epi! But this really creepy place – right up by the abortion clinic, as fate would have it; you were never far from a memory-mugging in a city this small – had been Kimbo's totally favourite place in the whole of B&H, the mentalist. It was the place she always ran to whenever we had a row – which, totally due to her clingy nature and unreasonably un-fun demands, was about every other day for the entire time we were together! – and the place she was always, when we *were* on speaksies, trying to get me to go to with her. 'Because it's the saddest place in town, Shugs!' Well, dude, don't go there then! 'But the most beautiful too!' Like, d'oh! – make up your tiny mind! Mind you, Kim was the kind that liked wallowing – 'feeling good feeling bad' and all that. Her favourite word was 'bittersweet' – I mean, what's that about!

Hmm, we'd see about bittersweet. I tipped Asif a slow wink, closing my hand over his. I wanted a shag; he wanted a museum; Ghost-features wanted bittersweet; everybody works! 'You ready to make a move then?' I was going to lay that ghost once and for all – at the same time as laying young Asif. BOGOF, in fact!

'Oh! – where are we going?'

'A museum, like you wanted to. Whatever my boy wants, my boy gets.' And to drive the message home I slipped my foot out of my shoe and ran it all the way up to his thigh, winking again as I did so. He choked on his Aftershock, bless him! And as we left the bar arm in arm, it was like I could see Kezzer-the-lezzer's holier-than-thou little pout of disapproval lurking in the corner near the karaoke stage. So I slipped her a sly wink all to herself over my boy's shoulder and threw in a little Sugar-smirk too.

Funny – part of me was flicking her the finger and thinking 'Screw you, Lewis!' but the even naughtier bit of my brain, which of course is my favourite bit, was thinking, 'Go on, girl, get a good eyeful – wish you were here? I do . . .'

'See the thing is,' I tipsily taught Asif as we stumbled up Ship Street on our way to the bus that would take us to sex-bliss via the Booth Museum of Natural History, 'that most of Brighton isn't very old, not compared with places like Lewes and Chichester. The original medieval town was mostly worn away by the sea and burned by the French, the bastards. But this bit, the Lanes, is one of very few surviving examples left in Britain of a Tudor fishing town. Good, innit!'

'So beautiful . . . so ancient!' Asif woozed, looking up and falling down.

'Steady on! – yeah, so the Lanes were due to be demolished in the 1960s because the council said they were like dirty, but there was this big fuss among the public and now everyone's dead proud of 'em. Great shops too! This one, Ship Street, is like probably the oldest.' I towed him on. 'See that there –' as I pointed into a well-posey window – 'that's Christopher Gull, Brighton's biggest dentist!'

For some reason he laughed loudly and nudged me when I said this, which bugged the fuck out of me because Kim had done exactly the same thing when I'd pointed that out to her as well. Will someone PLEASE explain to me what's so funny about that? I nudged him back, far less playfully, and he yelped as he fell into the gutter outside Jeremy Hoye the jewellers. 'And there's where Norman

126

bought Zoe's engagement ring – mind that lorry, it almost missed you!'

Only took us ten minutes on the bus from Churchill Square, though to be honest, as we got off I looked at the gloomy old place and wished we'd stayed there, cruising the mall. Didn't help that the place was in Dyke Road either; in the seat behind me, I could hear Ghost-Kiz snigger. Free entry too, which I always think is dodgy – I mean, who wants to do something which doesn't cost anything. Surely that means it's worthless?

I don't know what the phrase 'Natural History' had conjured up for me, but it was only full of poor stuffed bastards – birds, bears, you name it, in glass cases that ranged from the size of a telly to a few the size of a small car!

I gazed around me in awestruck horror. No wonder Kizza had been such a mis little madam if this was where she got her kicks – the Addams Family Petting Zoo! I peered at the big brown bear in the case by the entrance, and to my horror saw that a smaller bear was clutching at it. I read the label:

A MOTHER AND CUB SHOT BY JOHN
BADDELY IN MARCH 1881

'LOOK! – he's even gone and put his name on this monstrosity!' I hissed. 'What a right bunch of sinister pricks people were in the olden days!' I examined a large, shocked-looking bird in a case nearby, called the Great Bustard. 'And this poor bastard – Bustard, rather – he's got this look on his face, like, "Sod it, I've been stuffed!"'

Asif nodded thoughtfully. 'I think there was not the same respect for the animal kingdom in the past. People always say that our ancestors lived in harmony with nature, and that we do not, but I think it is probably the other way around.'

It was like being back at school! – dead things and lectures, NOT the ideal aphrodisiacs. I took him firmly by the arm and steered him deeper into the silent building. That was the one good thing about the place – apart from the poor dead buggers in the cases and the blokey on the front desk, it was deserted. 'Whateva! Come on, let's get educated!'

It was sad seeing the poor dead creatures, but they did have funny names some of 'em. 'Look!' I pointed at a moth 'That one's called the "Snout", and his mate's called the "White-line Snout" – bet we all know what he's been up to, eh? – doing the hokey-cokey!' There was a bird called the Buff-breasted Sandpiper, which reminded me of myself, and a Little Bustard to go with the big one.

And there, right in a little room at the back, there was a proper old 'skellington', as She and Evil call 'em. We leaned in to read the description:

NAME:
HUMAN BEING (HOMO SAPIENS)

RANGE:
WORLDWIDE

STATUS:
WIDESPREAD AND DANGEROUS

'Bit judgemental, innit!' I commented. 'Speak for yourself!
And it's a bit hypocritical, them having that poor baby bear
and his mum shot, and then going "Ooh, we're all so dangerous!" I wouldn't kill no animal!'

'But you have slain my doubts about adoring you!' Asif
smirked.

'Puh-leese!' We sniggered and I mock-fainted against
the case the skeleton was in. It didn't so much as shudder
– made of strong stuff, like me!

I look at that skellington, all old and cold, and then at
Asif, so young and warm; I heard Kim's footsteps in
another room, searching for us, determined to spoil our
fun, and then I heard my own breath in my ears. I leaned
back against the big glass case, pulled my skirt up and Asif
against me, and away we went – celebrating life against a
boxful of death.

But wouldn't you just know it? Even as I heard myself
going yes, yes, yes! I could hear that other, prissy little voice
going, 'Oh no!' So Asif got laid – but the ghost didn't.

Not this time.

15

Dirty deed done, we wandered back into town, drawn like moths to the mall. At a corner shop I stopped to get some fags, and blow me – or rather them – down if Ags and Bags weren't plastered all over the front page of the local rag! Right long hold-my-hand-mammy faces they had on them, and as far as I could remember it was the first time I'd seen their faces together without at a smirk on at least one of them. So at least I'd wiped the smile off.

But the smile was wiped straight off mine as I read what it said.

HATE CRIME VICTIMS 'DESIGN FOR LIFE'

Just weeks after their latest collection was completely destroyed in an unprovoked attack on their Clifton Hill home, celebrated Brighton-based fashion favourites James Agnew and Andrew Bagshawe fought back yesterday the way they know best – proving decisively that the scissors are mightier than the sword.

Both local and national press were yesterday given a sneaky peek at the shape of fabulous things to come at a charity ball, hosted by gorgeous local celeb, TV news reporter Marcella Whittingdale, at the Hilton Brighton Metropole. Showing what the proud pair described as an 'amuse-bouche' of flamboyant new pieces at the DESIGN FOR LIFE luncheon – which helps underprivileged young people learn to accessorize, thus improving their employment prospects and life choices – the courageous couple said, 'We absolutely refuse to be forced back into the closet by these bigoted bullies – who no doubt have totally pants dress sense and committed this heinous crime out of sheer envy! Instead we're going to press ahead, as planned, and fill that closet with absolutely fabulous creations!'

The pair, who are partners both professionally and privately, had planned to show their complete new collection – entitled 'Council Couture' – next month, but a vicious attack left their clothes – and dreams! – in tatters. Police are calling the vandalism a homophobic hate crime – which rose more than forty per cent last year – and are calling on anyone with any information about the attack to come forward. Additionally, the couple are offering a substantial reward.

'Wankers!' I yelled.

The shopkeeper gave me evils. 'Come on, love, we're not a lending library – you gonna buy that or what?'

Buy it? Burn it, more friggin' likely! Too right it was a bloody hate crime! – I hated the way that fat, rich pair of ponces thought they could treat me like trash and get away with it. And now THEY were playing the victims! This was Brighton, anyway – if there was a homophobic gang hell-bent on trashing the home of every rich, shirt-lifting local, it wouldn't take long to catch 'em, heh heh; they'd soon be checking themselves into A & E with overwork and exhaustion!

'Cept they wouldn't – cos it was me – and now I'd committed a hate crime, on top of my previous – and the police were looking for me . . . again . . .

And there was that bloody reward . . . and the fact that young Master Trulocke always had expensive appetites and a big mouth.

I threw the paper down and marched up to the counter.

'Twenty Marlboro Red. And two four-packs of them Half-Sugar Bacardi Breezers – Crisp-Apple flavour. And a bottle of Smirnoff,' I added as an afterthought. This wasn't the sort of problem that was gonna be solved by a handful of alcopops.

I slammed out of the shop and straight into Asif, waiting patiently for me outside. 'Don't you have a church to go to?' I snapped.

He looked hurt. 'I came here from Crawley just to spend today with you. I thought that was what you wanted – to make me a tour, and to be with me. Do you want me to leave you now?'

'Just carry these, will ya?' I thrust my bottled bounty at him. 'And don't say nothing till we get to the beach.'

We walked in silence down to the shore, and it wasn't till we were sat shivering on the shingle, and I had two Smirnoff-supplemented Crisp-Apple Breezers down my neck that either of us spoke.

'Asif . . . you know I'm not what they call a "nice" girl, don't you?'

He looked awkward. He wasn't keen on lying, due to

his religion and all that. 'You are nice to me. You are nice to animals.'

'Yes, but you know what "nice" means, don't you . . . it doesn't mean "kind". It means, "Doesn't have sex with people she barely knows."'

He looked away, picking up a pebble and throwing it. 'You know me. You know me well.'

'I don't even know your birthday!'

He turned to me. 'You know where I come from. What has happened to my people. That means much more than a silly birthday.'

I held his gaze. 'You're not keen on lying, are you, Asif?'

He nodded, looking uncomfortable. He knew what sort of thing was coming; maybe he knew me better than I thought.

'So . . . when you're with me, what do you tell your parents you're doing?'

He looked away again. 'I tell them the truth – that I am with a friend. The best friend I have made since we left Pakistan.'

'A best friend you fuck! – is that what you tell them?'

He flinched. 'Of course not! They would not think to ask.'

'So you just miss out the bits you think mummy and daddy would disapprove of, is that it? Very honest!'

He swung round and caught me by the wrists. 'What do you want me to say? To swagger into my parents' home and say, "Mum, Dad, I am going into Brighton now to screw my friend Sugar"? Would that be a good way for me to talk about you, do you think!'

'So . . .' I knew I was going to be really mean to someone who'd never done anything to deserve it, but I couldn't help myself, I felt so mad, bad and sad ' . . . if you DID tell Mummy and Daddy about me, how would you describe me, do you think?'

He thought about it – that is, half about what he really thought of me and half about what he thought I wanted to hear. He was so transparent he made clingfilm look like concrete. 'I would say she is very beautiful, she loves to laugh – but she is often sad underneath. And she seems very tough – but underneath, she is very vulnerable . . .'

That did it! – I friggin' hate that word! 'Vulnerable' – it's what wimpy men have to believe all women are inside no matter how tough they seem, or else they'll wet their Y-fronts in fear! 'Excuse me, Asif, but I think you'll find that it's a totally wanky misconception that girls who seem tough are all squishy underneath. There IS no "underneath"! Unless you're looking up someone's skirt,' I added rudely.

You'd have thought he'd have got the hint that I was somewhat displeased with his assessment of me from this tirade, but did he have the sheer smarts to back away from the spade? In a word, no. Asif decided to go for broke – as in 'if it ain't broke, break it'!

'And though she is often sad, I believe I can make her happy!' he blurted. 'Because I believe the answer to her problems is easy to give!' He took a deep breath – and then came out with the dumbest thing he could ever have said. 'I think she would make a wonderful mother one day – and I would like to father her children! And marry her, of course,' he added, bless him – as if I, who'd do it for half a toffee apple if you caught me at a weak moment, was gonna be offended!

Whatever, I decided – well, me and the Crisp-Apple Half-Sugar Bacardi Breezer chorus came to a joint decision – that this particular case of mistaken identity had gone far enough. I took the deepest breath a shallow girl can take and said – 'Well, I *am* a mother – but I don't know how wonderful at it my husband would say I am. Not that I've had much practice, seeing as how he ran off with my baby while I was in prison. That's right, banged up for stabbing a bloke with a broken bottle. Which, incidentally, is REALLY gonna count against me if the cops find out that I trashed my last employers' house so hard you couldn't tell if it was the right way up any more!' I smiled right into his horrified face and proffered my bottle. 'Bottoms up!'

Young Asif took me at my word here, leaping to his feet and rushing off down the beach without so much as a 'Here's mud in your eye!' – though no doubt that's what he was thinking, albeit in not the usual jolly spirit in which it's intended. But within a minute he was back at my side, staring down at me where I sat huddled, drinking and chuckling like a nutter on the cold hard shingle.

'So you are still married?'

'Last time I looked – yeah.'

He knelt in front of me and took me by the shoulders.

'Ooh, sexy!' I snickered. 'We gonna do it alfresco?'

'What happened when you tried to get your baby – what was it, a boy or a girl?'

'A girl,' I hiccuped.

'What happened when you tried to get your daughter back?' He was that bossy, you'd think he was a judge or something, not some teenage refugee cleaner!

I laughed, leering at him. 'Get her back! – why would I wanna do a mad thing like that! Jeez, you're as bad as my mum!'

He stared at me, gob open, like he was trying to work out what he's just heard, then when the penny finally dropped his face crumpled into an angry frown. 'At least your mum IS a mum! She did not abandon you like some . . . package in a park!'

For some reason this made me laugh uncontrollably.

'What is so funny about this!'

'What should I be doing?' I spluttered through my chuckles. 'Hunched in a bundle somewhere, weeping, because some bastard ran off with my baby? Who exactly would that help? Except you,' I added as a sudden insight. 'Who then might have less trouble coming to terms with the fact that he's doing the nasty with a heartless bitch who, it turns out, he didn't know one damn thing about after all!'

He sank down beside me, shaking his head. 'You can talk all you like to make like it's OK. I may not talk as fast as you – but I do know that it is wrong for a mother just to let her child go.' He laughed incredulously. 'And we haven't even talked about you going to prison for attacking someone!'

That did it. 'Attacking someone? Fighting back, you mean?' It was my turn to grab his shoulders now, and I'm glad to say I did it a damn sight rougher than he did to me. 'What if those little Christian girls taken off that bus and attacked and raped by those Muslim men had fought back, and had a broken bottle to hand, and stuck it in 'em while the dirty pigs were doing it to them? – would you condemn them too? Turn the other cheek, is it? Well, I'll tell you who always benefits from some people turning the other cheek – bullies and rapists and bastards in general! And I'll tell you who keeps on suffering because they've swallowed that shit about turning the other cheek – women and kids and Christians and sweet people, that's who! You put the two things together, and congratulations! – you've got a recipe for a really shit world!' I released him and took a swig of Smirnoff, washing it down with a Breezer chaser. Truth be told I'd forgotten what we were talking about and was play- ing for time. 'Well, go on then – you keep turning the other cheek, and see where it gets you!' I finished triumphantly if rather confusedly.

'Better to turn the other cheek than turn your back on your own child!' he came back. Ah, that was it. 'Though it may be a blessing if she never knows exactly what sort of woman her mother is!'

'Oh, make up your mind!' It was Kim and her mum, Stella, all over again, I thought: Kim's dad condemning Stella for being a drunk, a slut and a useless mother, and then moaning that she'd run off and left her kids! Surely if she, and now me, were such lousy rotten people, why would anyone want us to be bringing up impressionable young kiddies? Weren't we actually doing the responsible thing by letting these saint-like fathers take over parental duties? 'You bunch of fucking hypocrites!' Then out of sheer temper, I burst into tears.

Of course Mr Christian-Features saw this as his cue to detect the allegedly vulnerable little girl 'underneath' the hard-as-nails Sugar-shell. Like I was a frigging human M&M or something! Quick as you can say 'soft-centre' he had his arms around me, smoothing my hair and patting my back and stroking my arms like an octopus on a mission.

'Shh, shh . . . let it all out.' (Well, make up your mind, like, again.) 'I see how damaged you are beneath your shell . . .' (Like I was a tortoise somebody had stuck a sharp stick into!) 'How you are hurting deep inside . . .' (For some reason this made me think of cystitis, and I pulled myself away from him, making a real effort not to start laughing again.)

'I'm fine, Asif. Really I am.' I swigged from both bottles, which I'd kept a tight grip on during my enforced embrace. 'It's you that's got a problem with the truth, so far as I can see.'

He looked shocked, then resigned. I'll give him this, he had the sense to know when to stop this time. 'I see nothing will change your view, Sugar.' To my surprise he took the vodka from my hand and gulped hard on it before passing it back to me. 'But I will have my say finally, and then I will stop, and leave it to you to make up your mind.' He took my hands and looked down at them, then up into my eyes. 'All I will say is that to me, family is the most important thing in the world – more important even than my faith. But I feel so much for you, Maria, that I would be willing to make your family my own. Give me that, please.' Another swig of Smirnoff; how different it was when he did it – to make himself even more strong to do the right thing, not to make himself weaker so he had an excuse to do the wrong thing, like the rest of us. 'I am willing, if you want me to, to do anything we can to get your daughter back so we can be a family. And if my family in any way disrespects either you, your daughter or my decision – though they may not do so, I do not know – I am prepared to turn my back on them. Because then I will have a family of my own.' He smiled, and I knew what was coming, and whereas most other girls in my position would have swooned, I wanted to be sick. 'What is her name?'

'Renata. Ren.'

He smiled. 'I love her already.'

Right! That was it! I jumped to my feet. 'Well, isn't that just fucking peachy! Because now YOU can find Mark, I'LL divorce him, YOU can marry him, and REN CAN HAVE TWO DADDIES! After all, this is BRIGHTON!' And with that I stormed back up the shingle, cursing and stumbling all the way, a bottle in either hand – Picture Of An Unfit Mother.

*

It was a relief for once to get back to Sweet Towers. As I put my key in the door I could hear Susie, JJ and the twins laughing, and for once it didn't make me shudder with boredom, but cheered me up. Would it really be so bad, having Ren with me? It's not like I'd be on my own in some scabby bedsit – she'd have a grandma and an uncle and even two minging twin aunties. And a dad too, if that amazing display on the beach was to be believed.

And let's face it, my excuse for a career was hardly heading for the splashy smash of the glass ceiling anytime now; a new jiffy mop was just about the biggest thing on that particular horizon at the moment. How far had I got with my daring plan to get the hell out? Brighton held me as firmly in its grasp as some sort of camp Bermuda Triangle. Maybe it would just be easier – and wiser – to give in to what was expected of me.

My illusion ended the minute I set eyes on my family – not because they were repulsive, or rowing, or any of the usual stuff that makes you want to flee the family home and never go back. No, it's just that they seemed SO DAMNED HAPPY with what they'd got – so little, from where I stood (the doorway) – and with their roles of mum, elder brother and bratz. And standing there watching them, it was like I got a glimpse of my future, and how I could fit in too if I surrendered – older sister, old before her time single mum, pram-faced princess. And look, there's a 'ren' in 'surrender'!

I left the room quietly – no one noticed me. Which was fine with me, because I'd already decided I didn't want to fit in. Because giving in and doing the done/easy thing doesn't mean you're wise or grown up – it just means you're a coward. And I realized that though I was fond of my family and wished them no harm – even JJ, the little prick – I didn't actually want them to become the most important thing in my life. I mean, families are fine being the centre of your life when you're very young or very old because, let's be honest, you need them then and you ain't got much choice. But when you're living your life proper, they should be the scenery not the main event. Otherwise, in my experience, they feel like a straitjacket. And I wasn't ready for the nuthouse yet.

What I was ready for was bed. I let myself into my room and stared at the Twister duvet where Kim and me had had many a memorable roll around. For all her faults she'd introduced me to the idea that there was *something more out there*, given me a little taste of what a different life might be like – and it had tasted sweet.

I fell asleep on top of the gay duvet, and dreamed of chasing Ren through endless long corridors, crying. Only when I caught her, she was Kim.

16

I woke up in the morning full of beans – or at least full of Bacardi. You know those mornings you occasionally have when you know that you drank loads the night before and you can't work out why you have no hangover? Well, that'll be because you're still drunk, sucka! And the worst is yet to come.

So on the way to work I was grinning and singing to myself like a happy idiot – that old song 'The Only Way Is Up', for some reason – and it wasn't till fear and dread greeted me at the gates of Stanwick like two particularly ill-tempered bouncers that I really woke up and smelt the cleaning fluid. The only thing going up around here in the foreseeable future was the planes – with me not on them.

Asif was already there, pushing a brush around like some horrible illustration of Boy Going Nowhere – the perfect match for a pram-faced princess! – and studiously ignoring me. At break time the *Argus* I picked up just wouldn't let the alleged 'hate crime' die, and used the trashing of the collection as a springboard to a piece about all these horrible gay-bashing incidents that had happened in Brighton over the past year, which even though I knew weren't the same made me feel totally shady.

I couldn't believe it when I got home that night – I walked right in and there on the local news was Marcella Whittingdale interviewing Aggy and Baggy! She makes me spit anyway cos she's so gorgeous, but to see her nodding sympathetically as they piled on the agony made me want to hurl. I mean, sod all the other stuff going on in the world – clearly a few stained carpets and slashed curtains were far more important than people starving or being massacred.

To really rub it in, Susie, JJ and the twins were sitting there glued to the screen. 'Ooh, there she is! – look, Ria, it's that couple you used to work for!' squealed Susie.

'Couple of gaylords!' sniggered JJ.

'Oi!' tutted Susie. 'Leave it! – they've just been the victims of a hate crime!'

'My arse!' I spat. Immediately I caught JJ looking at me funny. 'What?'

'You left sorta sudden, din't you?' he said. 'Catch you drinkin' their booze, did they?'

This was a bit near the knuckle – I was about to make up some excuse when Susie said something incredibly annoying. 'Ooh, look at those clothes they've done! – they're a bit weird, but it's all the rage, innit!' She turned to me. 'Ria, you'd look lovely in 'em!'

I turned away quickly from the screen; I couldn't trust myself. 'Yeah, Mum, I can see why you like 'em – reminds me of that fancy-dress fairy-princess outfit you made me when I was seven. The one made out of twelve rolls of pink bog paper.'

She looked hurt. 'It wasn't my fault it tipped down and you were all in the garden!'

Of course it hadn't been – she'd stayed up all night attempting to work magic with a dozen rolls of Andrex

('Only the best for my little princess!'), and it wasn't her fault that the subsequent unseasonal downpour and ridicule was the first time it dawned on me that being pretty and sharp didn't count anywhere near as much in this world as having money.

I mean, it was bad when I was a kid, but it's got worse since then – becoming a model or, I dunno, an actress used to be a way for a hot girl from a poor family to get out. But now even those jobs are already taken, and you see the biggest dogs with famous dads just grab them as a matter of course. All that's left to us is to take our kit off – funny how those doggy rich chicks never want to be Page Three girls. Though I was dead pleased the other day when I read that some restaurant thought that Jade Goody was about to turn up, and they were all excited – and then it turned out to be Jade Jagger, and they were all dead disappointed!

About as disappointed, dismayed, disgusted, in fact, as I felt now watching Bag and Ag's latest, greatest fan – my mum! – ooh and ahh over them. This would be the same pair of stuck-up ponces who'd considered MUM'S ABORTION such a suitable source of inspiration, and who perceived council tenants as brain-dead breeding machines!

'So, James and Andrew, can you tell me more about DESIGN FOR LIFE?' the gorgeous Marcella was saying.

'Well, Marcella,' one of the loathsome blighters replied, 'my partner and I have always been interested in underprivileged young people –'

'That's a funny noise, Ria!' commented a twin. 'Like a piggy!'

'– chance to give something back –'

'Mum, look at Ria! She's making a face like she's going to be sick!'

' – give young people a helping hand –'

'Ooh! – maybe they could help you get some work experience, JJ! Ria, could you put in a word for your brother, do you think . . .'

'Oh, give me an effing break!' I slammed out and into my room, before I finally said something about having fixed their kiddy-fiddling wagon. And before I really gave Mum a mouthful about how dumb she was. It wasn't her fault after all that those two were bastards who'd give her underage son a roasting soon as look at him, any more than it was her fault the bog paper fairy dress had made me a laughing stock back when I was seven. I guess that was just the way life was . . .

I was just getting used to going down this 'whatever will be, will be' route for once when the bedroom door opened and JJ sidled in. He closed the door quietly behind him and then leaned against it, smiling slightly, his eyes heavy-lidded, looking at me; I know it sounds sort of sexy, but when it's your kid bruv, whose filled nappy you've had the pleasure of more times than you care to remember, believe me it's not. Besides, he was looking at me funny.

'What?'

'Nuffin.' He went over to my dressing table and started fiddling with my stuff – I hate that! And it's always just the one way round, have you noticed – I've never met a girl who goes into her brother's room, be it behind his back or right in front of him, and fingers his smelly socks and stuff. I'm not surprised that the world's full of men dressing up as women but not the other way round, and that it's nearly always men who want to have a sex change, not women – they're obsessed with our stuff! We're meant to have penis-envy – I don't think so – I think they've got punani-envy.

He gave himself a couple of quick squirts of, appropriately enough, my Envy perfume, and then turned to face me, smirking in a way that made me uncomfortable. 'So. Tell me again why you don't work for them two benders no more?'

'I got sick of skivvying, din't I?'

He snorted. 'Like you're not doing that at Stanwick!'

'That's different. There's other people there. It's a laugh—'

'Yeah, that's why you come home singing and dancing every night!' His eyes lit up as he saw some Benefit Bad Gal I'd lifted from Boots. 'Nice one!' Mouth wide open, he applied some as he gazed into the mirror.

'Do you know what a cretin you look?'

'Ta.' He put it down and blinked rapidly. 'Talking of which, you seen anything of Duane recently?'

A gay goose walked over my grave. 'Why would I? He's your mate.'

'No reason.' He turned around and gave me that look again. 'How much did the *Argus* say the compo was for turning in the kiddy that smashed up them gaylords' gaff?'

'I have no idea.' I jumped up and grabbed my coat. I had to get out before I let on that I was terrified he knew something and begged him not to tell. I had to get round there and lay it on the line to them – that they'd laid Duane, that is, and therefore it was gonna be their necks on the line if my guilt in this matter ever emerged. "Scuse me not spending the evening handing out make-up hints, but I've got places to go.' I couldn't resist a final dig; maybe if boys like my brother and Duane weren't so keen on lipstick, powder and paint, men like Aggy and Baggy wouldn't be so quick on offering them a quick spot of bed-bothering soon as look at 'em. It really pisses me off the way underage girls are always supposed to have 'asked for it' when some old perve screws them – there's no male equivalent of 'Lolita' is there? Though in my experience most boys would probably do it with mud from the age of thirteen onwards, they're that horny a lot of the time. 'Try to remember to put the tops back on, won't you – don't want 'em drying out or they'll be useless next time you got a hot date!'

I was furious as I stormed up Clifton Hill. The idea of being banged to rights by those two preening queens, my mother being amazed and ashamed and – the final straw – my thieving brother making free with my Juicy Tubes made me see it was time for action. Such as going right round to said queens' pit and making it clear as crystal that if they didn't let this business die down soon, I'd make damn sure that it wouldn't be Marcella Whittingdale giving them a shoulder to cry on, but rather *Crimewatch* feeling their collars. We'd see how much the local heroes they stayed when they were fingered for threesomes with minors!

I got up to their poxy door, thought about kicking it, but instead I did the decent thing and rang the bell. I could hear it echoing through the house, and almost like hearing the voice of someone you used to be in love with unexpectedly, I got a real flashback of how big and dark and plush it was, filled with the ghost of that scent – L'Heure Bleue. Well, this should have been *their* blue hour – but like a pair of slippery eels in a Teflon pan perched on a duck's back, everything had just rolled off of 'em. If anything, they were even better placed now! – the *Argus*, Marcella, local heroes, charity, bravery.

It made me mad. I rang the bell again. And this time, for good measure, I kicked the door too. And yelled, 'Oi! Gaylords! I know you're in there! Woss wrong, got your mouths full?'

And I kicked it again, harder this time. And grabbed the handle and rattled it hard, while yelling about what a pair of rotten bastards they were.

Because in spite of what I'd done to them and their precious house, I still hadn't rattled them. They still weren't scared. And it made me think of that old saying 'An Englishman's home is his castle' – in the olden days it was probably meant to like imply to all of us who live in this country, but, uh, I DON'T THINK SO! It's always a man whose home is his castle as far as I can see, and it's always a man in specific postal districts too.

Because though the thing in front of me was just a big

old door that opened straight on to the street – not even a porch door for protection – it made me think of when we'd been taken to Arundel Castle on a school trip one time. In the olden days the rich had had drawbridges and moats and stuff to keep the poor people out, but today they didn't need more than an intercom and a Big-I-Am attitude. Where I'm from our places get burgled and trashed all the time – and if they do catch the skank that did it, even to some old person that had nothing but the skin on their Horlicks to their name, what does the ponced-up judge do? Pat 'em on the head, give 'em an iPod and tell 'em not to do it again! Even if they messed on their antimacassars! But let a rich person's castle be done over and it was all posh hands on deck, hate crimes being announced from every rooftop and practically a price on my head.

I couldn't go back inside . . . I just couldn't . . . me inside that cold, hard detention centre and them all tucked up cosy inside their warm, cosy house . . .

'Why don't you pick on someone your own size, you fat bastards! – come out here and fight me like men!' I con-tradicted myself wildly, banging and kicking at the door. 'And leave my mum out of it!' I added for good measure. 'And you can shut your fat yaps about that bit of interior decorating I did for you the other day, unless you want me to come back with my mates and some spray cans and do the outside to match! And unless you want to make it back on to the front page of the *Argus*, but this time it'll be your little tea-parties with teeny-boppers, not your so-called charity work!' I was screeching now, conscious I was out of control and could be heard by any random passer-by, but I just couldn't resist a final volley of abuse. 'Talking of charity, you wanna keep bigging it up! Because that's the only reason a fit kid like Duane would have anything to do with you two, for sure! I'll give you fucking hate crime – it's you that must hate people, inflicting your disgusting bodies on 'em like you do!'

A curtain twitched – but it wasn't theirs. It was next door, and of course it weren't no ordinary lace curtain, not in Clifton Hill – it was one of those dyed black lace ones like that mate of Kate Moss's makes and flogs for a fortune – seen 'em in *Heat*. And then a window opened and a man looked out, one of those men who'd be half fit if he didn't look like he had a permanent kipper under his nose. Like Jude Law or Preston from *Big Brother*.

I realized I was going to be jail-meat pretty soon if I didn't do a bit of damage limitation. As I stood there peering back at old Jude-features, it did dawn on me that probably this wasn't my smartest move ever – returning to the so-called 'crime scene' and throwing alleged 'verbal abuse' at the absentees.

'Hiya!' I waved at the Law looky-likey. 'I'm just collecting for, um . . . Tourette's sufferers!' I grinned broadly and took a step towards him. 'Would you like to make a fucking contribution, you twat?' That'd do! Sure enough he pulled down the window with a look of absolute horror and I took off down Clifton Hill at a trot.

17

What had I done *now*? All it needed was for Jude to ring the cops and tell 'em that some really fit horny chick had been banging on the Bag-Ag door and threatening them with further damage to property, and all roads in Brighton led to me!

But let's be sensible here, I reminded myself. It was far more likely that he'd tell the gruesome twosome about it rather than squeal to the fuzz. And even if their suspicions were confirmed about my culpability, I still couldn't believe that they'd actually be so dumb as to point the finger or press charges – I mean, to be crude about it, I knew where those fingers had been, and what they'd been pressing, and it definitely wasn't legal, let alone honest, decent and truthful!

No – the weak link here was young Duane; weak link, missing link, whichever way you sliced it he wasn't the thickest doorstep in the loaf. We'd already established that easy livin' was his number-one priority; you don't become a fag of convenience with types as loaded and loathsome as Bags 'n' Ags for the good of your health, so he must've been getting a backhander every time. So what was to stop the dimbo trying to get his mitts on the reward money, without it occurring to him that by giving me the key he was an accessory?

I pulled out my mobile and called him. No answer.

'Duane, it's Shugs. Need to see you. Give us a call.' As I stuck my phone back in my bag I saw the Whitehawk bus and jumped aboard.

Approaching Duane's mum's house I reminded myself not to lose my rag again – imagine doing it twice in one day, from the white Regency houses of Clifton Hill to the council estates of Whitehawk; from riches to rags, shouting the odds all the way! So after ringing the bell, stepping back, checking the curtains for movement and finding none, I settled for scribbling a note and sticking it through the letter box.

DUANE – GIVE US A CALL. WE HAVE TO TALK – SUGAR

Well, they say that what goes around comes around. 'Sugar – we have to talk!' Asif hissed in my ear at work the next day.

I fixed him with a stony glare and shook my mop at him. 'Go on then – Chummy here's all ears.'

'MARIA!' He caught me urgently by the arm. 'I saw those men on the news last night! That you have wronged! That you must put right!'

'Talk to the mop – the moppet ain't listening.' I dipped my trusty pal in the soapy bucket, wrung it out and we were off, accidentally on purpose slopping dirty water all over Asif's shoes.

'But, Maria! . . . to make a hate crime! You know what I have been through, because of hatred.'

'Listen, Asif.' I leaned on my mop and glared at him. 'I've got every sympathy for you and your people and what you've been through at the hands of those crazed nutters back in Pakistan. But two nasty rich gayers having something spilt on their carpet is hardly rape and murder, is it!' I resumed my mopping. 'But don't let me stop you. You want to go round there and comfort them, go on and give them a treat. Go round there and turn the other cheek – butt cheek, that is. Mind you, don't take it too hard if they don't welcome you in with open arms – you are a bit too old for 'em, after all.' He looked blank. 'They're kiddy-fiddlers – child molesters.'

Now he looked absolutely horrified. I couldn't help laughing. 'Then you must go to the police immediately and report them for this awful crime!'

'Make your mind up! What are they – victims, or villains?'

He backed away, mumbling something about the world being turned upside down and turned inside out. A bit like the fate that would have awaited him, probably, if he'd gone round there all wide-eyed and opened-mouthed to comfort that pair of perves. I only hoped he felt suitably grateful to me for saving his arse.

But they say there's no rest for the wicked. I was just sitting down for a quick fag when the Dracules bowled up looking like they'd lost a silver bullet and found a sprig of garlic. 'Cept they didn't even look like Goths any more, even though they'd just arrived and were in their street clothes rather than their uniforms. And all the metal had been removed from their numerous piercings – they looked like a pair of human sieves.

'Can we go outside, Sugar?' Mr Munster muttered, and I noticed that the little fang implants were missing.

'Sure thing, Drew.' I grabbed my fags and grinned at him.

'It's Josh,' bustled Drina, and I saw that her novelty gnashers had gone too.

'OK, Drina!'

'It's Katie!' fussed Josh. Jeez, this was gonna be fun!

Identities firmly established, we went outside and found ourselves a choice bit of concrete, where I could look at the most beautiful sight in the world – planes taking off, carrying people escaping, if only for a short while. I lit up and squinted at them in the winter sunlight. 'So. How's tricks? How's little Bela doing?'

'IT'S LUKE!' they chorused as one. I obviously wasn't too hot at the name game today.

'OK . . . Luke it is. So what's on your mind?'

They got either side of me and made me start walking, darting paranoid glances all over the place. It was like being in a crap old spy film. 'We saw the *Argus*!' Josh eventually muttered. 'About . . . what we did that day! And the local news!'

'I know! – if they keep it up at this rate, there's gonna be a Hollywood blockbuster about it by Christmas. Bags me gets played by Angelina Jolie!' I jested, in what turned out to be a doomed attempt to lighten the mood.

'This is no joke, Sugar! It's not funny!' hissed Katie.

I stopped still, pulled my arms from their grasp and glared at them. 'With all respect, nothing ever is to you lot, is it! Bloody Goths. Why's everything under the sun have to be a fret-fest?'

'We're not Goths any more,' Luke boasted. 'We had an epiphany.'

'Ooh, really . . . you can get stuff from the chemist for that these days, you know. No script, straight over the counter!'

'SUGAR!' Katie grabbed me and shook me. In a feeble sort of way. 'Stop treating everything as though it's a stand-up routine! When are you going to grow up and . . . smell the roses!' she ended, again feebly.

Josh took this as his opportunity to come on all Dad. 'What Katie means, Sugar, is that this . . . incident, which we were stupidly involved in, has been something of a wake-up call for us. So we're going to grow up and accept our responsibilities as married humans, and as parents to Bela . . . Luke, sorry!' He yelped as Katie gave him a dry slap on the back of the head.

'But we still have a lot of time for our religion,' Katie continued, shooting him daggers, 'and to be a pagan, at the end of the day, is about being kind to people –'

'What about the "Wicker Man"!' I protested. 'They wasn't being kind to no one – they was doing human sacrifices left, right and centre!'

'Oh, stop nit-picking, Sugar! The point is that you made us, Josh and myself, complicit in a hate crime!'

I couldn't believe this. 'Hang about now! When the

three of us were romping about slashing shit and pouring crap everywhere, what did you think was going down? Did you think we were doing a bit for *Extreme Makeover*? Or a spot of spring cleaning, perhaps!'

They did look a bit sheepish here, and I took advantage of their retreat to press home my point. 'Look, it wasn't a hate crime – it was revenge. It wasn't attacking – it was defending. Like, um . . . Frankenstein's monster . . . when them peasants with the sticks on fire tried to murder him for summat he never done . . . or did he?' I mused. I swear, sometimes I think I should have been an intellectual – I'm always thinking. Still, I suppose you can't be an intellectual if you come from a council house.

'SUGAR! Stop avoiding the issue – and stop thinking you can lead us up the garden path talking about Frankenstein,' Katie tutted. 'We're just not interested any more. There's only one story we're interested in – and that's the one you're going to tell the police if you get caught.'

It took me a minute to twig what she was saying. Then I laughed, it was so silly. 'Oh! – you're trying to find out if I intend to grass you up.' I laughed again with real pleasure and confidence. 'No, we don't do that where I come from. That's the last thing you've got to worry about.'

They looked well relieved, like they'd both taken off shoes three sizes too small at the same time. And now they felt safe, of course, they could afford to care about me, or at least pretend to. 'But what about you, Sugar?' simpered Katie. 'Aren't you scared they'll tell the police it was you?'

'Not really.' I caught their arms in mine and started

walking us all back to the building. 'Seeing as how we've got a mutual friend. A fifteen-year-old mate of my brother's that they've been playing Strip-Twister with. I doubt they want that getting out – unless they fancy a bunch of peasants with sticks on fire going round and doing a damage to their precious house that'd make what we did look like a quick go-round with the Shake 'n' Vac. In fact –' I held the door open for them – 'I really can't imagine why they went to the cops in the first place, knowing that I know what I do.'

Josh swept through, Katie following him, and sniggered over his shoulder, 'Publicity, Sugar! Before this, they were just empty-headed rich micro-celebs. Now they're heroes. What's a few carpets compared to that! You've done something for them that no amount of money could buy.'

I gaped at him in complete and utter amazement; this brain-dead ex-Goth had seen right through to the meat of the matter in a way that had totally passed me by. So it was even worse than I thought; I had been screwed two ways by those fuckers, first as a phoney friend and second as a sworn enemy. And if Duane decided to cross over, that'd make it a hat-trick. I'd never be able to hold my head up in this town again.

But on the other hand, he had stuff to lose too – like my brother, he may have been fond of playing with make-up and walking with a wiggle when it suited him, but no way was he gay. I had to get to him, look him in the eye – one aspiring failed petty criminal to another – and make him realize how rubbish it was going to be for all of us if he squealed.

After all, I would lose my liberty. But once it got out that he had been the paid plaything of a pair of dirty old men on a semi-regular basis, he would never get laid by a hot girl again. And when you're fifteen, that's a whole new level of punishment. Sweet!

18

The next few days were like some mad game of kiss-chase organized by the – what's their name, them mad policemen always bumping into shit – the Keystone Kops. Asif followed me around shooting me lovelorn glances with eyes so cow-like I felt like slaughtering him and eating him between two bun-halves with cheese on top and a side order of salsa. Meanwhile I sought the elusive Mr Trulocke, lurking around every skatepark and graffiti wall in town, not to mention the benches above the walkway on Madeira Drive, until I felt like an ocean-going kiddy-fiddling perve myself.

Would you believe it, at the start of the second week I randomly came across him at a bus stop in Churchill Square, cruising for an ABSO with his poxy posse. He clocked me the second before my hand shot out to grab the collar of his school blazer, and tried to hustle his way on to the bus that had just pulled up, but an old lady hit him in the shins with her walking stick and he fell back yelping. His gnarly mates boarded the bus jeering and pointing at him. 'Collared by a girl! – dude, you're such a dick!' one of them yelled before the bus pulled away, leaving Duane bleating on the bus-stop bench, nursing his shins like a right royal wuss.

I eyed him coldly. 'Don't look good, does it D, letting a girl get on top of you.' Beat. 'Boy, how much harder would they mock if it came out that you let an old man get on top of you! Or two,' I added for good measure.

He scowled, rubbing his leg. 'Leave it out, Shugs – I'm dying here!'

I held out my hand to him. 'I thought you'd be used to taking punishment from senior citizens by now. Come on, let's go for a walk.'

We crossed the road to the Pizza Frita stall in front of the mall and I bought us a slice and a Coke each. We went and sat on a bench, and watched the language students flirt with each other in an international language they needed no phrase book for.

Duane washed the last of his slice down with the last of his fizz, burped appreciatively and said, 'That was the bollocks! – better than "Get in the car!" and a bullet in the head like in *Goodfellas*!'

'The only Goodfellas you and me are ever gonna get close to is the kind that comes in a box and has mozzarella on top,' I said, finishing mine up too. 'Damn! – whoever thought up frying 'em was a clever bugger!' I lit up a fag, sat back and inhaled happily. 'Now. To business . . .'

'Gis one!' Duane snatched at the pack.

I slapped him sharply. 'Paws off! – you're not old enough. Still,' I continued sneakily, handing him one, 'I s'pose that's a bit like locking the stable door after the horse has bolted.' I sniggered. 'Whore, rather!'

It was all psychology, see; I was being good cop, bad cop, carer and cusser, and the poor little tosser didn't know whether he was coming or going. I lit his ciggy and narrowed my eyes. 'But I guess if you're old enough to screw, you're old enough to smoke. And you're old enough to do business with too . . .'

'Fire away!' he coughed.

'Duane.' I took his clammy little hand and gave him a well-sincere look. 'Unlike the goodfellas of the non-edible kind, we're not criminals. Well, not really. I might have spilt some stuff on someone's carpet . . . but then, you might have let a pair of perverts do you three ways and got paid for it, and I think you'll find that could have you on record as a "common prostitute" for life.' I was winging it now, but the ignorant little prick wasn't to know that. I sat back and shook my head in a sorrowful sort of way. 'Look at you! – so young, so handsome, all your life in front of you, all that . . .' And I stuttered to a stop here, because for the life of me I couldn't imagine what lay in front of Duane – nothing good anyway. I mean, I'd intended to paint some rosy picture of his future all laid out before him – but even I'm not that good a liar.

He looked at me hopefully, waiting to hear how good it was all gonna be and, even though he was a little prick who used to perve over me when he should have been, I dunno, birdwatching or something, it almost broke my heart. Just because he came from some estate and didn't go to no poncey school, it was just so wrong that I had nothing to tell him about the way his life was gonna be.

'From ABC to Macky D in one accident of birth', Kizza used to say all sad-like about Ravendene kids, and even though I'd twisted her nipple for it at the time – which

161

she probably enjoyed, come to think of it! – for being such a mis-bucket, now I could totally see her point.

'JJ says you've got a lot of hot girls after you,' I improvised. 'But think. If you were by any chance to grass a person up in order to get a reward, then a person would naturally have to grass you up back, and what sort of reaction d'you think it would get from the hot girls, mmm? To know you'd been coining it by being a bitch yourself!'

He looked shocked, then looked away; I could tell that had got to him. I did feel a right cow, adding to his troubles, considering what a miserable little life I'd just foreseen for him – but me taking the risk of letting him add to mine wouldn't have helped him, would it, just landed both of us in it. It was each boy/girl for him/herself down here – and by 'down here' I don't mean Brighton.

He looked back at me, and he looked five years older than he had a minute ago. He looked hard, and on the way to somewhere harder. 'You din't have to say that, Ria. You din't have to threaten me. I wasn't gonna grass. Not on any one – specially not on you. Not after how you and your family been good to me since I was little.' He stood up, and looking up at him I didn't see a harmless, ignorant little boy anymore. Instead I saw a knowing, bitter young man. One who, for the first time, scared me. Just a little bit.

I tried to laugh the whole thing off. 'Duane, come on! – I never really thought you'd rat on me. I was just playin' you—'

'Yeah, you were.' He laughed, hoisting his rucksack.

'Look, don't go yet – you wanna hang for a bit? Have a laugh about the old times?'

'No.' He pulled out his mobile; he was already somewhere else even as he hit the button.

'We'll go to Threshers – I'll get you some voddy—'

'I can get my own – I'm a big boy now. Big enough for you to think I could grass you up.' He jangled coins in the pocket of his hoody and handed me 50p. 'There you are – that's for the fag. Keep the change.'

As I watched him walk away, I knew that I had won – but I also felt that we had both lost, and that we would go on losing, separately and together, because of the way the world was. Wherever there were rich young people trying not to feel old, there would be young people trying not to feel.

He wouldn't die of it – but he'd already grown up before his time. That was his punishment; whenever he met someone, from now on, he wouldn't see them as a potential friend or lover or general source of fun – he'd see them as someone to pay for stuff. Which meant that he was basically already a prostitute. A fifteen-year-old kid, already a prostitute.

You can call people gold-diggers and say they've got a choice in it and that, and of course you'd be right; I mean, this isn't bloody Thailand, no one forced him into it. And I'm not coming over all judgemental here – not after the stuff I've done! – and saying it's some sort of moral evil. All I'm saying is that seeing sex and money as having something to do with each other is going to leave you really short changed, somehow, sometime, somewhere down the line – probably forever.

I'm not saying it's going to rob you of your morals or your soul or anything hysterical like that – but it will rob a lot of the fun from your life. Because, and this could be just me here, it seems that we spend such a proportion of our lives working and hustling for a buck that the bedroom – or beach, or broom closet, or bench in the park after dark, wherever – is like one of the few places where we're just ourselves, just free. I swear I'm starting to be some sort of intellectual; probably started in prison, all those sleepless hours.

I've done some stuff in my life, violent and illegal and what have you, but I've never once been tempted to do it for money; drinks, yes, but drinks are the opposite of money, in't they – just gone in a split second, and bring you closer to the person that's buying them for you. Whereas taking money off them just pushes you further apart. And it sounds weird, but I reckon part of the reason I've never lost the plot, despite all the drama I've been through even though I'm still a teenager, is because I've always kept sex as my own private place to retreat to, where I can be my proper self, separate from the rest of the pushing-and-shoving world.

That's partly why I stabbed that guy on the beach that night – it was like he was trying to burn my house down or something, where I lived, and all I knew was that I sure as hell wasn't going to stand there – lay there – and do nothing to stop him. And to a lesser extent, that's how I feel about being offered money for sex; it's like you're letting someone rob you of something they don't have any right to. I know some girls, WAGS and that, are all 'Ooh, he pays for everything!', and they think they're so smart, and they think it's fun – but you're actually robbing yourself of real fun, real sex. At the end of the day, I think that if someone pays for you in the short term, you'll be the one who pays in the long run.

Fuck! – I laughed aloud in sheer disbelief at the fountain of airy-fairy thoughts my head was spouting. Was that a sermon or what! – it looked like Asif had been rubbing off on me in more ways than one. I needed a stiff drink and some hard shingle to toughen me up.

I walked down West Street, bought a half-bottle of Smirnoff and sat on the beach looking out to sea. I wondered if it was the same in France – people condemned to life being either hard or soft by an 'accident of birth', like Kizza had said. Or are they all snooty over there! I took a hard swig and considered the outcome of finally finding Duane. I was safe – but however you sliced it, Baggy and Aggy were safer: they were still sitting pretty, brave victims and charity belles.

So was this just the way it was meant to be, no matter how much you fought it? – if you were poor and pretty like me and Duane, were you just born to be fucked, and fucked over, by the rich and ugly? That's certainly the way it seemed from where I was sitting. And the old days were no better, from what Kiz had told me when she was off on one of her feminist ones – all them poor little pregnant servant girls screwed by the son of the house and chucked out into the snow; all them child prostitutes; Jack the Ripper! Boy, things don't change, do they! Except these days, since the gays came out of the closet and started pulling in the pink pounds, boys have to put up with being rich people's playthings too. Talk about come one, come all!

I thought about that magazine *Attitude* that I'd lifted a few times from Smith's on the odd day when I thought I might be/wanted to be gay; they didn't half make it look a lovely life, all about going out and getting mashed and lovely flats and gorgeous moisturizers. But then, right at the back – like a dirty little secret, miles away from the lovely life they show you in the rest of it – there're all these sex-lines, which are basically about shagging impoverished young boys. Sorry – 'lads'; obviously calling them 'men' would make them too threatening and calling them 'boys' not threatening enough.

It's not pretty boys with too much mince and mascara that the old gaylords lust after these days, apparently; all the vids are called things like *Paramilitaries, Council Estate Europe* and *Scally Boy Wankers.* Flogging the different chat-lines they've got obviously made-up quotes like, 'SEX WIV ME CHAV MATES: WHAT'S WRONG HAVIN' A BIT OF C**K FUN WIV A MATE YOU CAN TRUST?' – Robbie, 18. That'll be 'Rupert, 48' then, in some hot-and-bothered gay advertising agency in the West End of London!

I mean, I thought we were all meant to be proper PC

these days so gays didn't get offended – but it's not like they're PC themselves, is it! Not with sex-lines like 'Three prison inmates give me a good time', 'Soccer thug sex' or, worst of all, 'Let DSS bloke shag me for a crisis loan'. What next – shagging the homeless?!

Still, who was I kidding – if that sexy Dr Fox, say, wanted *me* to be *her* bit of rough, offered to set me up in a flat somewhere so long as I gave her Sugar privileges three nights a week, no way would I turn it down! As if that was ever gonna happen . . . I drained the bottle and flopped back on the pebbles, yelping as they hit my back. So now I was a hypocrite – the thing I hated most in all the world – as well as being broke, bored and on the wrong side of the law. Sweet – not!

Just then a text came through. I picked it up and squinted at it.

It was from Saz – the chief Fallen Angel from the airport. And an angel for real, for me, it seemed.

IBIZA GR8, STILL STEAMING, PARTY SAT NITE, CALL ME! R U READY 2 ROCK?!

Oh yes! – yes, I was.

19

Well, as I was saying, I may be a broke, bored, law-breaking hypocrite, but if there's one thing I can do better than anyone else it's party. And like the people who think the holiday begins at the airport – usually people I've had to sweep up the sick of at Stanwick – I think the party begins in the bedroom. On the other hand I'm certainly not one of those saddos who says that the best part of a party is a getting ready . . . hmm, someone can't pull/dance/be the sexiest girl at the party then!

Unlike me, I preened, as I gazed at the beautiful sight in the mirror while wiggling around to Gnarls Barkley with a bottle of Aftershock Black in my hand. Red dress plus shiny long dark hair plus gleaming caramel skin covering toned taut teenage bod equals perfection, in my book; I felt like reaching into the mirror, pulling my reflection out and giving it a good seeing to, that's how hot I was! To be honest, I wouldn't have minded my little ghost-girl turning up tonight, spooky as it sounds; it was at times like these that I missed Kim, I must admit. Kim: my portable, lovable and, as it turned out, shaggable little audience. OK – quit giving me evils – I know that we shouldn't think of our friends as audiences. But if they're staring up at us with adoring eyes full of love and longing, what else would you call them – tell me that!

*

I wondered what sort of mate Saz was going to turn out to be; whether she was going to roll over and accept Sugar Rules – in both senses of the word – straight away like a sensible girl, or whether she was going to put up a fight and jostle to be boss. I hoped not, for her sake; I liked the girl, I could use a new mate and I didn't want to have to go to the trouble of breaking her nose and/or her spirit before we became BFFAB – Best Friends For A Bit. But I *had* noticed the way she bossed little Vic around – so it was more than likely there might be a tiny bit of a power struggle ahead. Whatever! – I'd cross that bitch when I came to it, I decided as I took another slug of Aftershock and used the other hand to spray myself with Gucci Rush. In the meantime, she'd be a good wing-girl and hunting partner, so long as we weren't after the same prey. Which, luckily, it didn't seem we were this time at least.

Saz had happened to mention that the Fallen Angels had spent their time in Ibiza partying (in more ways than one) with the rugby boys they'd hooked up with at the airport. I'd been about to go into one about how she needn't rub it in, when I realized what she was trying to tell me – that Cameron, he of the fab abs and Calvin Klein waistband, was going to be there. Seeing as I wasn't on shagging terms with Asif this was just the news a girl wanted to hear, the cherry on top of the party pie if you like. Time to treat myself – and the sweet thing I fancied was going to be more than a minute on the lips but certainly not a lifetime on the hips. I was basically looking for a summer fling – albeit in deepest winter.

Course it was pretty much impossible for me to look anything but drop-dead gorgeous even going out for half a pint of milk from the Sikh shop on the corner, but a little extra attention to detail hadn't done any harm. After several hours in the bathroom, bathing, shaving and slapping on my stolen stash of Maybe Baby Benefit body lotion (heh heh, who was I tryn'a fool, more like Yeah, Baby, Most Definitely!) and taking a little trip to Brazil (ahem), I had stood there in front of the pile of stuff that counted as my wardrobe, biting my lip, trying to pick an outfit.

First big decision: underwear, or not to underwear – that is the question? On the one hand, I always loved going commando when I was a kid, but since going steady with Mr Christian it had seemed a bit in-yer-face – literally. And it's not much fun waiting at the bus stop in West Street after you've come out from a club, surrounded by pervy old geezers while the wind rips in from the seafront and you stand there like Marilyn Monroe on crack tryn'a keep yourself covered up – sort of defeats the aim of the object in the first place, which was to look like a raunchy slut who didn't give a damn!

Plus, if you don't put 'em on, how can anyone take 'em off for you? In the end it was this thought that made my mind up and I picked out a pair with laces at the back and bows at the side. Holding my dress up and surveying myself in the mirror, not to blow my own trumpet, but I reckoned I looked like just about the prettiest gift-wrapped present the world had ever seen.

'Better leave now or I'll get myself pregnant,' I snickered, blowing a kiss to the vision in the mirror and draining the remains of the Aftershock. 'Boy-toys of Brighton, let's be 'avin ya!'

In my experience there's two sorts of people that are always late to parties. There's the neurotic type, that seeks endlessly to prove to its sad little self that it's worth waiting for, and on top of that – due to its low self esteem – changes its clothes about twelve times before it feels able to leave the house.

And then there's me. I love an audience, and it makes more sense for everyone if they're all assembled and settled before the star hits the stage.

It was eleven before I found the big house in Tongdean – straight out of *Laguna Beach* with a big sweeping driveway, and I could see in the distance over the side gates a dirty great tree house in the back garden that would have easily housed the Sweet clan. There certainly was a lot of money in Brighton – a shame I always seemed to be on the outside, with my nose pressed up against the windowpane, while some jammy sod counted it on the other side.

I walked up the drive, rang the bell, whipped off my coat, stuck my tits out and smiled. The door opened and there stood Saz, all tanfastic from her holiday.

'Sugar Sweet!' She squeezed me tight, pulling me into the throbbing heat and noise of the perfect house-party in the perfect party house. 'Vic, look, it's Shugs from Stanwick Airport!' she yelled over her shoulder, then leered enthusiastically at me. 'Joined the Mile High Club yet?'

'More like Mile Wide, in that uniform!'

She laughed and Vic came wobbling up to us, very much the worse for wear. 'Candy! Glad you could come!'

'Sugar,' I kissed her. 'So'm I. Amazing house.'

'Parental shag-palace . . . should see 'em at it in the hot tub . . .' She shuddered. 'Sick bastards . . .'

'Don't start!' Saz warned her. 'Sugar's not interested in your dysfunctional family's idea of fun. From what I know of Sugar, there's two things she's interested in . . . let's get her a drink, and she can grab the rest for herself . . .'

They each took a hand and led me into the party, stopping to grab some tequila slammers a few times for sustenance. The house was a lush labyrinth, a right old house of fun with excellent entertainment wherever you looked. Downing my fourth slammer, standing at the crossroads of the opulently open-plan ground floor, I could see a bunch of boys trying to see if they could make a dozen miniature pizzas stick to the ceiling, and a bunch of girls snivelling along to a Dido song – and then girls wonder why boys want to be with their mates! It's called FUN! Then there was a boy surrounded by his older mates, who were encouraging him to down a bottle of some murky brown drink intriguingly labelled Yer Ho to much jeering and applause.

'Oh no!' yelled Saz. 'Not rum! It stinks!' She ran forward and caught the boy by the arm, pulling him towards the kitchen. He tripped, slipped, puked on to a pristine cream sofa and fell face-first into the steaming sludge. A huge cheer went up and the boy raised a hand to wave feebly.

'Tosser!' spat Saz, striking him harshly. She was obviously both the brains and the brawn of the outfit; while she was engaged in saving Vic's house from annihilation, Vic was more interested in banging on about her favourite subject – her sodding fiancé. I waited till she went off on a tangent in search of tequila and took the oppo to slip away and wander around this wasted wonderland in my own time.

There was a small dark room full of people dancing to Basement Jaxx Greatest Hits, loads of 'em in sunnies, clowns! – like if they're on something, who cares? Why bother hiding it, it's a house party for goodness sake, no parents or bouncers to get past here. Or often, when people do this, they're just trying to look like they're on something, which is the saddest of the sad. I ducked out and saw a semi-conscious girl who resembled an underage Maxine Fox – ooh! – being carried upstairs by some guy. Obviously knowing my own feelings for the fabulous Dr Fox I didn't really blame the perve for trying, but on the other hand it made me want to heave, reminding me of the times when I was younger, waking up and not knowing what had or hadn't happened to me.

Well, obviously I still liked the odd mini-break to oblivion, but after the blood-fest under the pier I was a lot more careful who I took along for the ride. And she DID look underage; I wouldn't be happy if people stood by while perverts took advantage of my little sisters a few years along the line, revolting as they might be now. So I sashayed up to him, did a double take and squealed, 'Max! What you playing at, girl!'

The bodacious Oriental chick was feeling no pain or surprise and mumbled something about feeling sick.

I fixed perve-in-training with a stony stare. 'Hello. I hope you've got a good excuse ready for taking my fifteen-year-old sister upstairs . . .'

He gaped: he could'na been more than twenty, but I could already see the future Dirty Old Man he was shaping up to be. 'Your . . . sister . . .' he mumbled, clearly confused.

'Adopted!' I spat, wrenching her from his grasp. She came without a struggle, throwing her arms willingly around my neck – even drunk out of your gourd it's got to be preferable to cuddle up to a fellow smooth-skinned, sweet-smelling teen sex goddess than a stubbly scumbag with nose hair so long he could use it as a comb-over if he went bald, let's face it!

He slunk off to find some other school-kid to sweat over, and I looked around for a safe billet where jailbait could sleep off her funk without fear of penetration. As luck would have it I saw Vic sitting with a pretty blonde-haired black girl on a big sofa, and by the incredibly bored look on the sister's face I needed just one guess on what the topic of the day was. I was sure a little diversion wouldn't go unwanted.

I hustled my zombie charge over to the sofa and lowered her down. 'Vic, do us a favour – my little mate here's had a rotten time with blokes recently – she's thinking of jacking it in and joining the pussy posse – tell her about your man and lead her back on to the straight and narrow, will ya!'

In her drunken euphoria, Vic was only too pleased to have a captive audience, and didn't notice that the girl was now well on the fast train to Noddington Junction. She threw a sisterly arm about her and, sickbag please, started in on how lovely Mr Wonderful's hair smelt. She had it bad.

The black chick gave me the thumbs up and melted into the party and I, all stoked up by my barely legal perving, set off to seriously look for Cameron. A girl for kicks, a boy for pleasure – a bottle of Aftershock for ecstasy! I'd sampled two already this evening, and now it was time to go for the hat-trick.

20

But just because I was on a mission, that didn't mean I'd lost my social conscience and stopped caring – oh no! From the living-room window I could see a group of kids, 'bout fifteen, sixteen climbing over the fence and heading up the drive. I nipped out and left the front door ever so slightly open to make it easier for them – I've always sorta felt it's my responsibility to help the younger generation get on in life!

As I set out on my X-rated expedition there was bass pumping out of several downstairs rooms at once, clashing in the hallway and bouncing back the way it came. I came across a small room already full of writhing bodies half out of their kit, but after giving the heaving monster mass a quick once-over, with practically no perving whatsoever, I soon clocked with some relief that the one I was on the trail of wasn't previously engaged. Be a shame to start a bloody, maiming girl-fight in Vic's parents' lovely house!

Then my attention was drawn by the yelps and shouts from the kitchen. Ever noticed how the main party action always seems to go on in there? Well, they say it's the heart of the home, although in this case it was less domestic goddess and more *Hell's Kitchen*, with a raucous amount of cussing and yelling that would have made Gordon Ramsay seem like a Trappist monk. And there at the centre of it all was what I'd come for, and it was fitting to find him here as ooh, did he ever look edible. He was certainly giving me an appetite.

You know sometimes in magazines you read these really lame-ass descriptions of sexy men: 'His eyes were deep blue pools', 'His hair was the colour of ripe corn', 'His arse was like a Krispy Kreme doughnut I wanted to take a dirty great bite out of', and all that sad gay crap? Well, when I looked at Cameron, I wasn't thinking about his eyes, or his hair, or his arse either. Having had an eyeful of his abs and given them a ten, I was now thinking about one thing and one thing only.

The girls were hanging off him like cheap bling, around a big old kitchen table, giggling and drinking. They were pretty – but they were nothing special. And I was going to give him a Sugar-rush he'd never forget. I had a sudden burst of inspiration, ducked back from the kitchen doorway and into the living room where I grabbed a bottle of Ketel One from a side table, and then sauntered into the kitchen.

He looked up like I was carrying my own spotlights – all the better to blind you with, boy! – and grinned gorgeously as I slammed the bottle down on the table. 'Wanna play?'

He shrugged the girls off. 'What's your game?'

I leaned down and across and looked at his mouth as I spoke. 'Snort it!'

'Snort it?' some drop-kicked chick sneered, rolling eyes that were well on the way to matching her red and white Topshop dress and looking at Cam for sad approval.

Course he totally ignored her and smiled at me with a sexy lift of one eyebrow.

'Show me, Sugar.'

I didn't need asking twice. 'Get us some spoons,' I smirked at the bloodshot bimbo. She did so, sulking but unwilling to show herself up in front of a boy she still thought she might have a chance with – poor deluded cow. The spoons were shared out and filled with vodka – there were eight of us – me, Cam, four adoring girls and two of the boring sort of boy who you always find hanging around hopefully where there's too many chicks fighting over one stud, kidding themselves they'll be getting some of the spare. Hmm . . . that might have been true back in the old days but these days the leftover girls are more likely to put on a bit of a lezzer show for the apple of their eye and see if they can't tempt him away from his original choice with it. I've seen that routine a hundred times – and let's be honest, I've even done it a couple.

But just like in those soft-focus, mushy old movies it was like there was just Cam and me in the room. 'Go on then, you first,' he teased. And so I did. And then, not quite so like the mushy old movies, I had a nostril full of vodka and a feeling like someone had just shoved an ice pick up my snout. I was tryin' not to gurn like a toothless farmer as the pain slammed round my head and my eyeball felt like it was on fire. Then came the equally attractive sniffing and running-nose moments and a feeling not unlike you get if you put your head under water at the swimming-baths and half of it goes up your nose . . . mmm, but then came the rush, and the giggles, and I stood there laughing like a loon, watching Cam battle his way through the same set of sensations.

And then we were giggling together and with our other partners in crime, who I REALLY, REALLY LIKED now and someone had grabbed the bottle and was topping everyone up for round two. Yeah it hurt, and yeah it was pretty horrible and it didn't really even get you all that high, but only a sadult would ever bother asking why we did it. If there was a reason, it probably wouldn't be worth it now, would it?

But as much as I was having fun, with all thoughts of Asif and Duane and the Clifton Two well and truly shoved to one side, I had better things, or people, to do than hang out in the kitchen all night. I leaned close and whispered in his ear, 'Do you fancy going somewhere a bit less private?'

He drew back, looking surprised. 'What!'

'The orgy room, or whatever it is . . .' I inclined my head towards the hallway, thinking of the dark, writhing room beyond. A carpet of fit flesh, no less, and a carpet I wanted to join in the laying of at that.

He didn't need to think twice – and who could blame him.

We were just getting down to it when Saz appeared in the doorway. 'Get your kit on, quick! – the police are coming!' We all jeered at her. 'Swear it's true! – the little jerk next door who complained about the noise earlier just came back to boast about it! – GET DRESSED, NOW!'

Well, say what you like about the youth of today, but they're a resourceful lot. And they don't hang about either. So when the fuzz did finally turn up, they were faced with the surreal sight of some fifty kids – the underage brigade had done a runner – all sitting round a game of Trivial Pursuit. Saz had even managed to find some classical stuff to stick on in the background, the kind of thing you get on those wildlife programmes Susie's so fond of where big bastard birds of prey are gliding over snow-capped mountains as Sir David A. bangs on about wingspans and how this is the last greater-titted eagle thingy alive in the wild. Makes you feel respectable hearing just one snatch of it, and I could tell it had the cops well fazed.

So anyway, there we were, fifty mashed-up teens, a Triv board and 'Nimrod' reaching a climax in the background – glad somebody was. Unsurprisingly, the two rozzers looked a bit confused. A cocky-looking kid with a floppy posh-boy mop and the eye-watering arrogance to match stepped forward. 'Can we help you gentlemen? And in return, perhaps you could help us – we're trying to establish which came first: Barbie Doll or Mr Potato Head? It's for a wedge – so please don't answer if you're not sure . . .' This was followed by (pretty unsuccessfully) suppressed laughter and a not at all suppressed retching noise. 'Nerves,' explained Mr Cocky. 'We take our Triv seriously up here in Tongdean.'

For a minute it looked like the younger of the two coppers, who I couldn't help noticing was a fantastically fit mixed-race kid, was going to bite, but his older, colder colleague did a quick sweep of the room and decided that losing his rag just wasn't worth the effort. None of us looked seriously underage, and he could take names and addresses till the cows or at least the parents came home, but most of the kids probably couldn't even remember theirs and or would just be makin' 'em up. He'd end up with a load of, 'No honestly, my name is Doherty, Pete Doherty!' and such, and if he bothered carting anyone off, chances are they'd only spew in the back of the police car that he had to ride around in all day. And you never really get rid of the whiff, do you?

'OK – just keep the noise down,' the nice dad cop said, grinning slightly. Obviously had thrill-seeking teens of his own. Hopefully they had a bit more sense than me, because before I knew it I was on my feet and talking back, giving the young cop loads of dangerous eyeballing. Well, I had just been getting to grips with Cam when we were so rudely interrupted – I was all fired up with nowhere to come, wun't I!

'Ooh, I don't know if I can do that,' I snickered. The fit filth's eyes were going right through me, which in my wasted state I took as a come-on. 'A bit of a screamer, me!'

PC Pulchritude – learned it off Kim; good, innit! – was undressing me with his caramel-coloured eyes now, so I licked my lips and stuck out my tits for good measure. 'Is that your truncheon – or are you just pleased to –'

Hotty whispered something to Dad, who nodded, both of them staring at me. 'Is your name Maria Sweet?' he barked back. Whoa! – my reputation had gone before me!

'That's right – but you can call me Sugar . . .'

'Can you accompany us to the police station, please, Miss Sweet,' said Dad pleasantly, stepping forward in case I wasn't quite sure if I fancied it.

Sod it! Aggy, Baggy and Squealer Trulocke! I'd been having such a blast that I'd forgotten all about them. Still, better go quietly; if I bolted, that'd be as good as signing a form saying, 'YES, I DID IT, AND I'M GLAD, YOU HEAR! GLAD, GLAD, GLAD!' Tell you what, I may have always thought that making an entrance was my speciality, but I think I may well be extraordinarily talented at making exits too. You could have heard a pill drop as I left the building, every inch the wasted star, with my police guard.

You've got to hand it to me – whatever the weather, I'm always up for fun. I just can't help it; as PC Sexy opened the door of the police car, I looked up at him from under my eyelashes and murmured, 'What – no handcuffs?' I couldn't swear to it, but I'm sure I saw some slight disorder in the bottom half of the law.

21

What do you know, I was home in a couple of hours! – and to rub it in, I pretended I was scared of being attacked by a perve and persuaded PC Hotty to drive me right up to my block. In Ravendene, that's like getting a scholarship to Oxbridge or Camford or wherever, and I was pleased to hear a little chick no older than nine say enviously to her mate, 'All the best shit happens to Maria Sweet!' She thought I'd been arrested, bless!

Hadn't been, though – just routine questioning as an ex-employee. Seems that B&A reported my little hissy when it dawned that it could glean them some good publicity, but too late for the police to get much evidence – style over substance once more, typical! They couldn't prove it so they had to let me walk – or rather, ride, with my very own uniformed chauffeur. And of course Bags and Ags had their own secrets they'd rather keep away from sunlight streaming through a courtroom window, if you wanna get poetic about it.

But it did have one not altogether unwelcome knock-on effect – I got the sack from Stanwick. According to Katie, who filled me in by text a bit later, someone at the cop shop told someone in Security that I was 'bad news' – well, if no news is good news that suits me fine, cos I don't wanna be no news. The way I saw it, things were getting icky with Asif and the boredom quotient was going right through the roof with even my former playmates the Drac-ules becoming solid citizens. Upwards and onwards!

I couldn't be arsed to be angry – this was the second job I'd lost through no fault of my own; this trying-to-be-a-sensible-girl thing wasn't working out so well, was it! I was more than tempted to sign on and goof off but I needed the readies for alcopops and Topshop. I spent a few days lolling about in bed, yelling at daytime TV and wondering whether to bother calling Cameron to finish what we started. In the end I decided to let it go – he was fit and everything, but I'd only just put one lovesick puppy behind me and I didn't have the patience to train another one. Eventually I had to admit it was time to get my sweet butt down to the jobcentre.

It was pretty grim being back there again, like the playlist of my life had got stuck on one song that just kept starting over and over and it was one of the crap ones they put on there for free that you never get round to wiping. Except this time I made sure I walked into that place with rock-bottom expectations. I even laughed when I realized the face behind the desk was my number one fan, the mus-tachioed monster who'd first sent me up the hill to the little house of the fairies. 'How ever-so-terribly lovely to see you again,' I chirped in my best prissy-missy Kim voice. I could tell by the dead-eye glare she threw back that she hadn't for-gotten me – natch. Then this mad gleam came into her eye and she shuffled through her cards with barely suppressed glee.

'Miss Sweet! – back so soon! Let's see what we have here

that might be suitable, shall we? Which of the many gold-plated career paths open to you it might be wise to follow!'

'What about lap dancing?' I suggested – not that I was desperate to show my gorgeous bits 'n' booty to a bunch of unappetizing perves but, let's face it, I'd earn more in one night there than I would in one week, fortnight or month in any number of 'respectable' jobs. By the savagely smug look on her face I just KNEW that the words 'bucket' and 'mop' were gonna figure in my new job description, and I wanted to get in there first with 'tassel' and 'thong'. 'Top Totty? Pussycat Club?'

She made this disgusted face like you'd have thought I'd inquired about the possibility of becoming a crack-smoking cannibal infant-school teacher. 'Really, Miss Sweet! – isn't that rather degrading? Surely we can aim a little higher than that—'

'If by aiming higher you mean on my knees scrubbing, no cheers – not again! And personally, I don't see what's so degrading about taking a ton tip off of some old pervert. Cleaning the toilet him and people like him piss all over, on purpose I bet, for fifty pence an hour at Stanwick – that's degrading! The other's just wealth redistribution.'

'Anyway, Miss Sweet, it's all beside the point. You're only seventeen.'

'So what? Isn't it better to do it now, rather than when I've got so much cellulite you could play draughts on my ass?'

She shuddered, cheeky cow! Whoa, I bet you could play Twister on her ass – in her dreams! – there was so much of it. 'It would be illegal, not to say immoral, for us to send a seventeen-year-old, however *worldly*, to an interview for a job in the sex industry.'

'It's not sex – it's entertainment! Least it would be the way I'd do it,' I sniggered.

She looked at me with narrowed eyes. 'The entertainment industry, you say?' She scrabbled away in her box – ewww! – before waving a scrap of paper excitedly before my eyes as if it was him out of Hard-Fi's phone number. 'Chilly!'

My first reaction was to look down at my chest. 'No, I'm fine thanks. They're always this perky.'

'No. Miss Sweet – C-H-I-L-L-I not Y.'

'Why what?' The old bag had flipped.

'Chilli, as in "peppers", and no, I don't mean the band.' She paused then and looked all smug; I actually think she was waiting for me to congratulate her on being so damn cool and down with the kids. S-A-D. When I didn't speak her face went back to its death-mask stare. 'Here – Chillis@Chasmeister, taking part in this year's Festival of Fiery Foods at the Marina. And they're looking for a "creative, energetic person" to represent them. Singing and dancing a plus.'

You know what – I'm so mindlessly optimistic that just for a millisecond I thought she was gonna cut me a break and send me to be one of them tequila-shooting cuties you get in clubs; not exactly a one-way route to the stars, I know, but plenty of free booze and easy targets. But then I clocked she'd said 'food festival' and remembered the look on her face when she'd said it and I just knew what was coming.

And that's how I came to be standing on the waterfront at Brighton Marina dressed as a giant chilli, on the hottest day of the year. Like I think I might've said before, even dressed in Dawn French's cast-offs I'd still tighten trousers at ten paces, but trust me, there's no way to sex-up six feet of morbid-maroon, curve-covering chilli couture. Funny, when you think about it, chillis are famous for making things hotter, but in this case, they were doing the total opposite.

It was my job to hand out flyers to the fiery-food crowd and invite them over to the stall where Chasmeister was doling out Hellish Relish, Four Bean Fire and other taste sensations to tempt would-be punters. Course, in my natural state I'd've had 'em queuing back to Hove, but dressed like an embarrassed carrot I was hardly fighting 'em off. I'd tried explaining this to Chas himself, but he'd just let out this big belly laugh and said, 'Honey, there's nothing hotter than my peppers!' Actually Chas was kind of all right, offering me food and drink every five seconds, and laughing at just about everything anyone said. But the job still sucked. Standing there being ignored by sadults, laughed at by the odd passing teen (like, if you're so cool what the fuck are you doing at food-fest? Loser.) and breathing in the ripening smell of whoever had worn the sad suit before me. I entertained myself for a bit by making kids cry (apparently the sight of six-foot foodstuff can be quite scary when you're little) but it was too easy and I soon got bored.

Chas came over and whispered in my ear, 'Show 'em your talent, Sugar!'

'What – get my tits out?! But there's kiddies!'

'No – the song!'

'Please, Chas – not the song!'

'Come on, Sugar! – then you can go and have a fag break.'

Screw it; might as well give it some welly. I stepped away from the stall, flung my arms out and sang:

'I'm a little chilli, red and long
Listen to my chilli song!
If you get your mouth round me
Not so chilly will you be!

I can make the Mitchell brothers' hair curl
I can melt a frozen turkey's heart
Put colour in the cheeks of any Goth girl
And bring a zing to every other part!

I'm a little chilli, red and long
None too sweet but oh so strong
If you get your mouth round me
There'll be tears, you wait and see!

Hotter than Saudi in July
Hotter than Angelina's guy
Hotter than a scalded rat –'

'CAT!' yelled Chas.

'Hotter than a hot potat
(O).'

'That's shit!' someone yelled. Well, it's one thing for me to critique myself, but I'm damned if I'll let a giant ear of corn diss me. It was that jealous giant ear of corn from the Foxy Furnace comestibles stall! – I'd clocked those useless bitches earlier, the twin bosses all done out in basques that were ten years and two sizes too small for them, smirking at every male in sight. And even dumber were their tame veg – an ear of corn, an onion and a gherkin, all pretending that they were hot stuff while shooting me evils. They knew I was the real deal, and they were determined to hate on me for it.

'Oi – corn-features – hate the game, not the playa!' I called good-naturedly across to her.

'What! – you, a playa! Looked in the mirror recently?' yelled back her onion sidekick, walking out from behind the Foxy Furnace stall to stand shoulder to shoulder with her yellow pal.

'Yeah, I tried but I couldn't see nothing cos your fat white arse was blocking the view!' Not being funny, but old onion-head was easily as wide as she was tall.

'Excuse me, bitch, but are you picking on my friends?' queried the gherkin, stepping forward to show solidarity with her minging fridge-mates. She had a loud, bossy voice – Roedean, I guessed. I eyed her warily – don't care what people say about Ravendene girls, those Rodders chicks have got a rep as the nastiest fighters in town.

'You're not in some sodding posh cocktail now,' I warned. A crowd of about twenty had gathered, at least half of them kiddies, and I wasn't about to go down in front of an audience, even if it was one against three. I could even see little Rajinder there, my sisters' Swearers Three sidekick, holding tight to her dad's hand and looking wide-eyed and upset! – great, it'd be all over the estate within the hour. I had to front it out here. 'You're back in reality, sweetheart. You wanna mess with the bull, you're gonna get the horns!'

'Oh really?' gherkin-face sneered. 'Well, bring it on! Cos at the moment, all I'm gettin' is bullSHIT!'

All the crowd sniggered at this; I felt my face going red, to match the rest of my ridiculous outfit. I couldn't let some posh cow and her vile veg mates get the better of me! – I had an image round my hood, and it wasn't as a defeated vegetable either. And they were mob-handed – I could be forgiven for fighting dirty.

I began to back away towards Chas's stall; the rotten roots thought I was chicken, and nudged each other, smirking.

'Not such hot stuff now, are you!' the gherkin crowed – then shrieked in pain as the huge handful of chilli powder I threw in the direction of her posh old face hit the target.

Well, it was a bit of a blur after that – probably cos of all the chilli powder flying around, not to mention jars of pickled onion, gherkin and corn. It was like a riot! – wrecked stalls, missiles flying, people running screaming for cover like somebody had let off tear gas! A couple of innocent bystanders even fell into the water, though thankfully no kiddies. And wouldn't you know some killjoy had to go and call the cops! Lucky I was already in disguise; I hot-footed it out of there before the first rozzer was out of his car – a fugitive pepper on the run!

Climbing the hill to Ravendene – I seemed to spend my life slogging uphill these days; Kim would probably have called it a metaphor – I had to admit it was pretty unlikely Chasmeister would want me back again for round two. It was so unfair – *quelle surprise*! I mean, I'd just given a brilliant example of the kind of work performance that Paris Hilton and Nicole Richie would be proud of in *The Simple Life* – except of course when they pissed about, jeopardising someone else's livelihood and getting sacked within the first hour, it was all one big reality TV money-spinning joke for them. For Sugar it meant another trawl through the job pages or a trip back down to Job Central; Mrs Moustache was gonna start thinking I fancied her.

I put my key in the door and immediately I knew something was going on. I could hear this sort of cooing noise, like a pair of pigeons being patronizing. And another sound that immediately unsettled me – like someone trying to talk – but too . . . young . . .

I walked into the living room and stopped still. Susie was sitting on the sofa, as usual. But there were another two people there – both of whom I'd met, but neither of them I could say I really knew. One of them was Catherine Wood, my husband's mother.

And the other was my daughter.

22

I stared at her, sitting there on the floor – a beautiful baby girl of eighteen months, with big brown eyes, caramel skin and straight, shiny hair; the darkest that brown hair can be without being black.

She stared at me – a giant red chilli pepper with blood and mascara staining its face in equal measure.

And she screamed, very loudly, and stood up on her lovely little legs and wobbled over to the sofa, burying her face in Catherine's lap and howling, 'Go 'way – GO 'WAY! NO, DAPPY – PANDA OFF! BUBBA CWY!'

Mum and Cathy stared at me indignantly.

'What?' I exclaimed. I edged towards my baby. 'Hello . . . Ren.' I held out my arms. 'Got a hug for . . . Mummy?'

She looked up, took in the giant bloodied vegetable looming over her and screamed at the top of her voice 'GO 'WAY, BAD PANDA!'

'She's scared of pandas,' Cathy explained.

'Do I look like an effing panda!' I spat, which of course started her off again.

'I'll take her outside for a bit,' Cathy said, scooping the screaming tot up. 'Show her the view from the balcony.'

'Leave the door on the latch, Cath,' Mum called. Then she turned to me. 'Well! Isn't this nice!'

'You're calling her Cath already!' I said accusingly.

'Since when were you so matey with my bastard ex's mum?! How long has this been going on?!'

At least she had the grace to look slightly ashamed of herself. 'We've been chatting on the phone for a couple of weeks. A month maybe. At the most.'

I just couldn't take it in; I lit a fag. To my amazement Mum grabbed it from my hand and chucked it out the window! 'What the fuck—'

'Language!' she tutted. 'There'll be no more of that, for a start. That and smoking. And . . . dressing up like a panda and frightening Ren.'

I tried to keep calm. 'Mum. I'm a fucking chilli pepper.'

'Well, she thinks you're a panda.'

'Whatever. The point is, she's got to get used to it.' I sat down wearily. 'What's going on?'

'Mark's been chucked in jail. In Saudi Arabia. Apparently he was handing out Bibles like they were sweets.'

I couldn't help laughing. You had to hand it to the boy I married, he was certainly something different. Couldn't go to jail for GBH like a normal person, no! 'And what am I supposed to do about it? You saw what she was like – she fucking hates me!'

'Well, you do look a bit frightening right now,' Susie conceded. 'But it's nothing that a bath and a bit of blusher won't put right. And if you're not a panda—'

'For crying out loud – I'm a chilli! They're nothing like!'

'Ren was scared by a panda on the telly recently, Cathy says – she calls everything she doesn't like "panda".'

Just as Susie spoke the last word, Cathy put her head round the door, Ren calmer in her arms. All it took was that one word – PANDA – and she was off again, screeching like a police siren.

'I think we'll be off now,' Cathy yelled over the racket, 'and try to make a fresh start tomorrow!'

'I DON'T S'POSE MARK MENTIONED MY IPOD, DID HE?' I yelled back. 'ONLY I'VE REALLY MISSED IT!'

'OK, Cath!' Mum yelled back. 'Come by around twelve and we'll go out and leave them to it!'

The door slammed and I stared at Susie in absolute astonishment. 'Please tell me I was hearing things then. TOMORROW?!'

'They're staying at a B & B. To give you two time to . . . bond. Reconnect. Have some one-on-one family time.'

'You've been watching too much *Trisha*, Mum.' I stood up. 'And from what I've just seen, it'd take a truckful of superglue to bond her with me!' I stomped out, slamming the door. Well, one of us had to be the grown-up, and Susie was obviously living in never-never land!

I woke up early next morning with a weird sort of Christmassy feeling; when I realized I was excited about seeing Ren, I was so freaked out I couldn't get back to sleep. I went into the kitchen; She-Ra, Evil-Lyn and even JJ, which made me feel annoyingly tearsome, were sitting at the table making these really crap cards with TOO OUR NEECE written on.

'You've spelled that wrong, for a start,' I commented over JJ's shoulder. 'It should be A-R-E – OUR.' The clown only rubbed it out and started again! I turned to Susie. 'D'you think Ren's gonna get the Sweet brains, poor little cow? Not that the Wood ones are anything to write home about, judging from the situation Mark's landed himself in. Bibles in Saudi! – the pigs don't even allow the letter X there, cos it's too much like the cross.'

Susie looked at me amazed. 'How d'you know that, love?'

I didn't really feel like telling her about Asif right now. 'Never you mind.' I looked at her sternly and held the door open. 'Outside. Now.'

We went into the sitting room, and immediately she launched into a justification of the farce – albeit a rather exciting one – about to be played out. 'Ria love, I was only thinking of you – you said you wanted to get her back. You were gonna get that private detective, remember? Well, she's here now, love, and . . .'

I was about to launch into one about how I never said I wanted her back. In fact she only had to check with Asif (not that she'd met him) to find out I'd been pretty damn vocal on that point. But then I remembered I had kind of agreed to find Ren, just to shut Susie up, back when she was going on about the need to hold another baby in her arms and all that crap. And I'd never bothered to set her straight that the only baby girl I'd given much serious thought to tracking down was Kizza.

Susie was looking all wounded-puppy-dog eyes at me now. 'It wasn't easy, Ria, you know, getting Cathy to agree to this day-out idea. She was all, "No disrespect to your daughter, Mrs Sweet, but are you sure she's capable of looking after Ren by herself? Ren's been through such a lot with her dad being taken away, and I couldn't stand her to suffer any more." Took me a while to persuade her that that was exactly why Ren should be with her mum. I mean a baby needs to be—'

I'd stopped listening a couple of sentences back – so that sanctimonious cow, who had aided and abetted my ex to run off with both my baby and my iPod, thought I was incapable of looking after my own daughter, did she! 'Susie, it's fine, no worries. Course I wanna spend the day with her – can't wait. It'll be sweet – loads of catching up, loads to do. Quality together time . . .'

I clocked the stunned look on Susie's face as I buzzed out the door, back to my room to get ready. I'd show them. I sat there on the unmade bed, shaking and slugging away at my stash of voddy until I felt my heartbeat get back to something like normal and my hands stop trembling. Yeah, I know, if the thought of being left alone with Ren for a day spun me out so much why hadn't I just told them where they could shove it? Or easier still, just agreed to it all then buggered off outta there till the whole thing had blown over. They didn't expect me to be any good at it, so why bother trying? But that was the whole point, Mark's patronizing mum with her, 'No disrespect, Mrs Sweet.' – bitch! But course what she meant was no respect as in she had none at all for *me* – and for some reason that made me want to show the old cow she was wrong. For one thing, if she was such a shining example of good parenting, how come her pride and joy had walked out on his darling wife, breaking up their family and depriving his baby daughter of a mother's love and then, just to make sure he really screwed things up, gone and got himself banged up in some foreign jail? I might not have been mother of the year, but at least I wasn't pretending to be.

And in the last few weeks I'd been disrespected by just about everyone, from a couple of child-molesters to a sodding gherkin, and I wasn't about to let my bastard ex's mum join the list. I finished the vodka, stood up and held my head up high. I'd never won a prize in my life – but I was ready to win my daughter.

I'd like to report that I was wrong, for once, and that Ren threw her arms around me and clung with all her little might when she and Cathy came calling. I showered, slapped on a bit of fake tan, flowery scent and pink lippy and sallied forth to charm my daughter. But as luck would have it, I also pulled on my favourite monochrome shift dress – black and white striped, with black opaques and white shoes. As I opened the door with the broadest and most welcoming of motherly smiles, I realized that I could be mistaken – if only by an easily excited eighteenth-month-old child – for a –

'PANDA!'

'Oh, for fuck's sake!'

'LANGUAGE!' tutted Mum and Cathy as one, as I huffed off and changed into Susie's second-best dress so Ren could put her sticky hands all over me without me having an epi. See, I was a natural at this mother stuff! Didn't seem to make much difference though: the minute Ren reset eyes on me, her little face crumpled up and turned bright red, and she was wailing into Catherine's neck before I even opened my mouth.

Cathy prised her off and held the bawling little bundle out for me to take. She was only wearing a sort of grey smock frock with a picture of a gurning teddy bear on it! – what's a panda if it's not a bear in its PJs, I ask you! And she had a really filthy bit of blanket in her hand, which obviously she'd been using as a hanky or something. It was totally rank and I felt smug that Mark's mum obviously wasn't as perfect a mother-substitute as she liked to make out.

'Here you are, Maria. And this bag has her things in it . . . Ren, love, Mummy's going to look after you today . . .'

'PANDA OFF!' She kicked her legs, hitting me in the mouth.

'Fuck off!' I exclaimed instinctively.

She stopped kicking and stared at me with her big hot-toddy eyes. Then smiled hesitantly. 'Panda off?'

'Off!' I agreed, nodding like a nutter. 'Off, *off, OFF!*'

It was a small thing, but sadly all we seemed to have in common for now.

Cathy saw her chance. 'OK, Maria, we'll be back around six. See if you can get her to sleep by then, but if you can't, no worries.'

'Bye, love – don't forget to take the twins' old buggy out!' called Susie as Cathy pulled her away.

Ren stared wide-eyed at this betrayal, from me to where her grandma had stood and back again. For a moment I thought I had her – and then the door closed. Between glass-shattering screams the poor panda-hating little scrap called for her daddy, her granny – anyone but her mum – and as I stood there holding my squirming, crying daughter in my arms, I felt as lost and scared and abandoned as she did.

23

Still, nothing ventured, nothing gained. What do kiddies like? – telly! I carried her into the living room, singing the theme from that *Tots TV* show that the twins had loved at the top of my voice –

> *'I'm a Tot*
> *Je suis une Tot!*
> *Tilly, Tom and Tiny*
> *We're the Tots on Tots TV*
> *One, two, three – boo!'*

She seemed to like this; at least, it stopped her howling. And it had French in it too, which'd be useful when it was time for her to chat up language students like her mother before her. It's good to be bilingual – and no cracks about me and Kim, thank you; this is a little kiddy we're talking about!

As this bit had gone down a treat, I racked my brains for another song from the show and came up with 'Tom's Trumpet' –

> *'Follow Donkey all the way home,*
> *He knows where we're going.*
> *Follow Donkey all the way home,*
> *He knows where we're going.*

We got lost all on our own,
Now home is where we're going.'

But, pathetically, I felt a lump in my throat at the 'We got lost all on our own' bit, and it must have communicated itself to Ren, because she started crying her little heart out twice as bad as before.

What else did kids like? – softies and snacks! One thing about Susie, she always has the fridge crammed with tasty and nutritious scran. I juggled Ren on one hip, feeling like an Italian earth mother out of a pasta ad or something, and bent down to investigate. Of course, the first thing Ren saw was a bottle of the Panda Pops cola the twins threw back like water, and the crying gave way to wild screams of 'PANDA OFF!' once more. I slammed the door shut, but not before grabbing a packet of Cheestrings; kids couldn't get enough of these, in my experience. And cheese was just milk that had learned to stand on its own two feet anyway, so naturally it was good for babies.

Where should I sit her while she had her snack? – she'd fall straight off the chair. Then I saw the twin buggy that Mum had held on to in the hope she'd get lumbered again. I sat her down in it, strapped her in before she knew what was happening, unzipped the Cheestrings and handed them to her. She looked astonished but not sad, so I took advantage.

'That's it! – clever Ren! Now, darling, you sit there like a good girl and eat your nice lunch while Mummy puts a nice DVD on.' I scooted into the front room; luckily there were loads of old tot-orientated ones that the twins had long outgrown but Susie didn't have the heart to get rid of. Best vet them first to make sure none of them had a bloody panda in; I selected a *Postman Pat* and dodged back into the kitchen to fetch Ren.

Bless; she'd got the Cheestrings and, instead of eating them, hung them all over her little head. Some hung from her ears like manky earrings; some hung down over her eyes like a really badly peroxided fringe. She smiled angelically at me, and what was left of my heart seemed to melt like a Cheestring left on a radiator.

'There's a clever girl!' I clucked, running up to her and grinning like a loon; I was really good at the 'unconditional love' thing too, it seemed. 'Shall we go and see Postman Pat?' I wheeled her into the living room, pushed the buggy right up against the screen and pressed play. The familiar theme song started up, then just when I was congratulating myself at the length of time I'd managed to keep her happy – must've been at least five minutes since she last had the abdabs! – the wail went up –

'NOOOOO! – ICKLE PANDA! OFF, ICKLE PANDA!'

It was only stupid Jess, the sodding black and white cat! I turned it off straightaway. 'There you go, baby, nasty panda's gone!'

'NASTY PANDA!' heaved the poor little mite – and that's when I realized that she had actually eaten some of the Cheestrings after all, as they shot out of her tiny mouth and all down Susie's second-best dress. How clever of me not to have worn my own clothes!

'GRAMMY, GRAMMY!' Ren was wailing now. For a minute I was well impressed that she knew about stuff like important music awards at such a young age, but then I clocked she was crying for Cathy. I know it was only natural, Cathy having been around her for so long, but I still felt a flash of jealousy. 'Specially when she started up with, 'DAPPY, DAPPY!' That'd be the Bible-bashing jailbird who stole my iPod and made my baby a stranger; thanks, you bastard, I'm SURE that's what Jesus would do!

I decided to get her out and about; as things stood, there seemed a lot less chance of running into a panda than there was inside. And that was a whole nother tale of woe. When Ren'd been tiny, we'd had this sort of dinky doll's pram and of course I'd had Mark to help me; alone, with a big baby and a double buggy, it seemed like a particularly punitive sort of novel deterrent to the high rate of teenage pregnancy in Britain. Boy, if they showed you films of this in school, forget STDs, this'd have all the little girls keeping their legs crossed! Of course, the lift wasn't working, so I had to fold it back down again while holding a howling Ren in one arm, then carry it and Ren down five flights of stairs, the buggy bumping against her legs and covering my gorgeous caramel gams with bruises. If there's one thing I hate, it's bruises that weren't any fun to get; they're probably what Kimmy used to call an oxymoron.

Outside of course it was raining, so I had'ta get Ren under that plastic cover thing before heading off. Where to go with a baby that age? – too young to take shelter in the cinema, and anyway chances were some pixelated panda bastard would come prancing on and unleash the forces of chaos. We could trail around the shops, but I didn't have the spending cash to buy anything and I was a teen mum with a big buggy – Security would be watching me like a hawk, which with my recent brushes with the law was the last thing I wanted.

So in the end we went to Macky D's, sharing a Happy Meal. And you know what, for a while it did what it said on the box; looking at her, so seriously chewing her chip with her tiny front teeth, I felt a massive wave of love and pride.

Well-off, well-fed, well-smug types, like Jamie sodding Oliver, see teenage mums like me sitting in Macky D's feeding our kids chips – and straight off they feel totally free to make these judgements about us, in a way that if a person made judgements about, say, a black kid just by looking at them, they'd be run out of town as a racist. But they know nothing about the way we live. They're not even smart enough to realize that we feed them chips NOT because we don't know that there's these things that grow on trees and taste dead boring called fruit and veg, but because we want to see our kids *smile*. Because soon enough we know the smiling's gonna stop, when they find out that because of the address they call home and where they went to school, everything in life's gonna be loaded against them. We buy them Happy Meals because we want them to be happy. And we know there's a strong chance they're not gonna be, even if we stuffed them full of fruit and veg till the cows the Happy Meals are made of came home. Which obviously, they ain't gonna!

All that non-stop crap Jamie and his followers spew up about what mindless evil sods poor parents are for not stuffing salad down their brats' throats till it comes out through their tear-ducts! And saying that where you get in life can be changed by what you eat. It's just a total stinking big fat lie! The simple fact is that you are not what you eat. You are where you're born, you are how rich your parents are, you are where you went to school, what you are lucky enough to be handed on a plate. Fair play to his little girls, but no matter how dumb they turn out to be, they're going to have a lovely life, cos their dad's rich. And no matter how bright Ren turns out to be – well, let's not bring the party down, shall we!

All of a sudden I felt like crying, and I didn't want to spoil things when I'd only just got her to stop. So to take my mind off it, I put these two chips in my mouth like fangs, and I rolled my eyes back in my head. And you know what? – she may have had a cob on about pandas, but even at eighteen months she didn't give a toss about vampires – or zombies. That's how brave she was. My brave little girl. Just like me.

And I thought how if Aggy and Baggy came along right now, how if they looked through the window they wouldn't see the beauty of me and her sharing our first lovely moment together – they'd just see the cliché, a deadbeat mum and a doomed daughter. Because despite all their airy-fairy arty-farty alleged creativity, they simply had no imagination. All their life there'd be beauty right in front of their eyes and they wouldn't recognize it, because it was ordinary beauty. Aggy, Baggy, Jamie Oliver – it was easy to have a good time when you had hard cash and big expectations. But we, Ren and me, were having fun on chips and thin air – and that was something those stuck-up pricks would never be able to achieve, never in a million years.

'I love you,' I said.

And sweet as you like, she smiled like a baby angel and puked a massive mouthful of watery ketchup right down her front. She looked down at it, and laughed in amazement, her big hot-toddy eyes engaging mine in what looked like pure delight. I laughed right back – it was the *exact* colour of watermelon Bacardi Breezer!

'Just like your mum, intcha! Well, we'll see . . .'

And then the sun came out.

I couldn't keep her laughing forever – but I could keep her laughing for now . . .

'Come on,' I said, getting up. She lifted out her arms to me, and tears came to my eyes. 'Let's have some fun, before they stop us!'

24

Kizza used to say, when the sun shines all roads in Brighton lead to the pier – not the sad old ruined one, but the big bright brash one. The old West Pier is the one we sit on the shingle by and stare at when we're determined to look on the dark side and bang on about the death of love, time 'like an ever-rolling stream' bearing all her sons away and all that Indy crap. But the Palace Pier is the place our feet take us to when we come to our senses and admit that, generally, however hard life gets, there's always candyfloss to be spun and fun to be had. So naturally that's where I took my Ren, for our day in the sun.

She was gurgling as I wheeled her down West Street – a Happy Meal indeed. But when we got to the bottom of the hill and she saw the sea the gurgling stopped and she turned back to look at me with this amazed 'What the fuck!' look. I was so proud that she was looking to me as an authority, that I began to talk softly to her as we crossed the road to the Esplanade, even though I've always thought that women look totally dumb doing that.

'That's the sea, darling, isn't it lovely? Because you were born here, in Brighton, and your dad and me used to bring you down here when you were very tiny. Then I had to . . . go away, and so did you. But now you're home again, where you belong.'

Jeez, where did that come from!

Of course, we couldn't go on any of the pier rides, even the teacups; she was too little. But it felt like a ride in itself, albeit a very quiet and tranquil one, pushing the buggy slowly along the boards of the near-deserted pier, seeing the sea glint beneath us and hearing Ren's gentle cooing as she took it all in. As we stood looking out towards the Marina, a seagull came and landed on a pier post nearby, doing that weird sideways look they give you, trying to suss out if you're carrying grub on your person. It reminded me of the way Kim used to sidle up to likely lads when I tried to get her to score pills for me off strangers on the seafront, and I laughed.

To my delight Ren laughed too, kicking her legs and waving her arms at the gull. 'NAUGHTY – NAUGHTY! OFF, NAUGHTY!' I was impressed that she didn't call it a panda – see, already I was having a good effect on her!

I wheeled her through the flashing lights and kerching-ing machines of the pleasure dome, and out the other side past the Victorian fish and chip restaurant where they played those songs that sounded happy but were really quite sad, all those songs about being taken away from home like 'It's a Long Way to Tipperary'. We stood at the end of the pier and looked up wide-eyed at all the scary rides, and I thought they were nothing compared to the one I was on. I lifted Ren out of her pushchair, held her up so she could see what a big wide world it was and quietly sang her a song I'd only just remembered:

'I have a little boat and her name is Gloriette
Across the brave horizon her prow is boldly set
Gloriette, sail away, to where your fortunes lay
Then come back safely 'cross the bay.'

Ren looked thoughtful, then blew a raspberry. We both laughed in sheer delight.

'That's my girl!'

I started crying then so quickly strapped her back into the buggy, turned around and set off back in the direction I'd come. Story of my life. I started wheeling her along the seafront pavement in the direction of Hove until we came to the Pirates Playground and paddling pool.

I knew I'd made a mistake the minute we sat down. The place was full of those posh old birds who like to think of themselves as Yummy Mummies; the kind of old broads who look right down their noses at young single girls who invest in looking good, and dismiss them as bimbos. But then they're so desperate, they even have to make having kids something that adds to their sex appeal! Like the tots are tiny pimps or something. As for that MILF crap – yuck! They started that themselves, obviously. It's like, 'I may have a kiddy and be staring the menopause in the face, but I'm not slack, honest!' My arse!

It's meant to be 'chav' parents that are loud and sweary, but these broads broadcast every boring thought they have at the tops of their voices; all that mindless crap about how child-friendly France is, and how dyslexic kids are actually super-bright rather than thick, and how the additives in oven chips turn people into serial killers. It's like they think they're being permanently watched by some CCTV camera that's doing some perfect-parenting test on them. Well, from where I was sitting, they were far from perfect; one of them was responding to a pre-school brute, who was repeatedly screeching at the top of its voice, with a tinkling laugh and a ceaseless, 'That's a lovely scream, darling! – can you do it again, only louder this time?'

Another was leeringly droning, over and over, 'India, do you want to do a wee? Do you, India? Want to do a wee? Or would you rather do a poo?' And though they, the mums, don't swear, the kids themselves have filthy mouths – the boys are often perverts. Rather than curtail their creativity or whatever, the mums let them run riot; one of them here, called Rory apparently, was running around with his nasty little cock out shrieking, 'Look at my willy, isn't it silly!' – in front of little girls and everything! And all the stupid cow mothers were just laughing appreciatively! Then one of them started breastfeeding a dirty great 'baby' big enough and ugly enough to open beer cans with its teeth!

Me, I was staring at the rapist-in-waiting Rory through narrowed slits of eyes, just daring him to come over to me and Ren and show us his manky miniature dick. The little shit obviously had a death wish, because eventually he capered right up to us and waved his nasty chipolata right in Ren's amazed face. 'Look at my—'

I moved so quick I surprised myself. Before he could say the offending word I had him by the throat and was hissing in his face, 'If you don't put that dirty little worm away, I'll yank it off and stick it so far up your bum you'll have an umbilical cord. There's ladies here –' and with this I rattled Ren's buggy so roughly she yelped – 'and I don't care how your slag of a mum's brought you up, you don't do that in front of ladies!'

With this I jumped up, grabbed the buggy and high-tailed it out of there. I wasn't scared, not of what a bunch of wusses like that would do, but I suddenly couldn't stand the way I felt about them. Not the hate or the repulsion – that was easy and familiar and enjoyable. No, this time there was envy too – cos of Ren. Don't get me wrong – the last thing I wanted was for her to grow up like those posh prats India and Rory. But I wanted her to have the freedom that they had, to choose what they were gonna do with their lives. And what choice was she gonna have growing up on Ravendene, with me as a mum?

As if on cue, to remind me of my shortcomings, she vomited her Happy Meal all down herself. At the same time a seagull dropped a message on my head. It was a proper wake-up call.

'Come on,' I said. 'Let's get you home. Proper home.'

Susie looked like she might try and change my mind when I announced that Ren should stay with Cathy, but then she must have seen my face, really seen it, and made the wise decision to keep her mouth shut. And it wasn't like she could never see Ren again. Now Cathy knew I wasn't going to try and keep Ren I reckoned she'd be happy to visit a bit more often. When she took Ren away, I lay down on my bed to have a think. I could hear Susie and the kids tip-toeing around. But I wasn't feeling sorry for myself – far from it. Rather, I was feeling I'd done the right thing. For once.

I'm not pointing the finger here – that sort of life was fine for some people. My mum had always wanted the life she had, basically – OK, she'd probably have chosen to have a bit more money and a man who stuck around a bit longer than his sperm did, but she had always wanted to have kids young and have a family around her – hence her insane recent desire to conceive yet again, and our eventual trip to the abortion clinic when she realized that the economic practicalities were beyond her. (How long ago that seemed now!) But that just wasn't me, and it never really would be. And even if I could have made a wish and made myself like that, for Ren's sake, I wouldn't have. That was the truth. I cared about myself more than I cared about anyone else – and the idea of changing that seemed like suicide. I reckon being big enough to know I'd be a crap mum was about the best parenting skill I had. (Irony or something, Kizza would have said.)

So I didn't care enough about her to stick around – but I did care enough to get her out of here. Course my little ghost-girl Kim was never far away from my thoughts here, forever banging on about her lousy relationship with Stella. But when you really thought about it, I reckon Stella did Kim a big favour by screwing a toy boy and sodding off to the Bahamas or wherever. I mean, yeah, it was Stella's behaviour that had sent Kim off the rails and yeah, some of it had been bad, like when Kimmy OD'd, but loads of it, most of it, had been sweet. Instead of following the safe and trodden path to Dullsville she'd been diverted to somewhere a whole lot more exciting. She'd stopped being scared of every little thing that might mean she wasn't the perfect daughter and instead she'd thrown herself into life (and my arms). She might have got a few bruises but so what? They weren't fatal. If Stella had been a 'better parent' Kimmy's life would probably have been a whole lot smaller and duller and, come to think of it, so would mine. Well, I wouldn't wish that for Kizza, or for me, and not for my own daughter. If you ask me, that's love.

25

I don't know – I got quite sad after that. It was like I slept for a hundred years. And when I finally woke up, there was only one place I wanted to be – on the beach, the only place you can still go when no one else will have you. I took an old Bratz notebook down there, and a big fat joint, and I vowed to myself that I was gonna stay there till I'd sorted my life out.

But sad to say, I smoked it straight down in about six seconds and fell into a reverie about Bratz. I know it's childish, but I just couldn't get over how unfair it was! They totally had, between them, the future I wanted. You can jeer and say get a life – but how could I, when a bunch of plastic dolls already had it! I was sooooo like Cloe and Co.; jealous mingers called me a slut cos I was so pretty, nobody knew exactly what my racial origins were, and when I'd had a few too many drinks I couldn't spell my name properly either.

Why couldn't I just hang out being fabulous, like what Bratz did, and get discovered? Nothing else seemed feasible or made sense, to be honest. I could just imagine what the audience on *Trisha* would be yelling at me by now: 'Go to college!' 'Get some qualifications!' 'Do something with your life!' They make it sound like the simplest, most straightforward thing on earth – but I mean, who's zooming who? It's like I said about Jamie Oliver's kids – you're not what you eat these days, you're where you're born. And for people to pretend that if you put your shoulder to the grindstone, your nose to the wheel and all that crap, you'll 'make something of yourself' all above board – well, they're liars. Because the only thing you're ever going to make of yourself by following the old rules is seven sorts of cretin.

To kids of my generation, from my background, the idea of becoming, I dunno, a doctor or a teacher or something 'worthwhile' seems about as likely as becoming a unicorn, only not as sexy. I mean, if you were a unicorn you could at least make some money from it; be in a reality show or something. You keep hearing ugly posh people tut-tutting that girls today have no ambitions beyond being a WAG, a pop star or a topless model – but that's because those are *realistic* goals if you're young, good-looking and poor. Nothing else is.

That's why so many girls like me have babies – so they've got an excuse to give up a fight they've already lost before they begin. Of course if I'd kept Ren I'd have a total excuse not to work. But what a lousy reason to have a kid! That's one of the reasons I knew I couldn't keep Ren: cos I wasn't ready to give up yet, and I wasn't ready for her to give up either. I wanted her to stay with Cathy, to be taken out of the loop, to think there was more to life than being a WAG or a glamour model. And if you think that makes me a hypocrite – well, cool, kiss my gorgeous ass! 'Cept you couldn't afford it – and you'll never be able to afford Ren's either if it turns out for her like Cathy plans it will.

But what did I want for ME? At the end of the day, the thing was that I didn't want to lead an ordinary, boring, respectable life – but I didn't want to live a beat-up criminal one either. I guess I wanted what Kim used to call *la vie Bohème* – breaking the rules but somehow getting away with it. Sounded pretty much like what I thought of as my balcony in the sun. Talking of which, I was *still* no closer to it than when I got out of prison with my fat arse and my heroin habit.

So now I wasn't going to be a full-time mum I was back on the job market, 'cept for me it didn't promise to be much of a shopping experience; it wasn't so much of a market as a manky old blanket on the pavement with a few bits of knock-off that no one really wants. If I'd stuck it out as a chilli, who knows, maybe I could'a worked my way up the food chain and one day made it to a singing sandwich or a dancing dhansak, but I figured that after starting the full-sized food fight my career as a performing vegetable was pretty much over. Bothered?

If I was going to make a splash I really needed to do it soon before I got old and wrinkly and couldn't remember that I once wanted a thing called 'A Life'. So with a heavy sigh I picked up the bloody Bratz notebook and made another list of things for and against me.

FOR
Total goddess
Just about still 17

AGAINST
No money

No job

No prospects

Then a couple of strange things happened. I was gonna write down 'No boyfriend' in the FOR column, young, free, single and all that, but then I realized thinking about Asif made me feel sad. I knew I didn't want to be with him, but I realized I did feel kinda bad about how I'd left things. It wasn't really him I was mad at, he'd just been in the line of fire after B&A had sent me into one. He could be annoying, and let's face it we'd never see eye to eye on the whole happy family thing, but we'd had a good time, me and him. I'd been calling the shots from the first moment I saw him standing there holding his broom handle, and all he'd done was his best to keep up and keep me happy. And all of a sudden I was back thinking about Kim again. The other person who'd done her best to keep up with Sugar and failed. And almost like that spirit writing you hear about, I found myself writing in big letters under the AGAINST heading, NO KIM.

And so it turned out that that was what I wanted after all – Kim. Came as a bit of a shock, to say the least. OK, so I know like, dhur, I think about her loads and even imagine her ghost following me round Brighton, and I know what we had was something good, and special. But honestly, until right then I didn't really know how much I wanted it, wanted *her*, back. I guess I'd thought it was just nostalgia or whatever, but now I knew I just needed to find her. I stared wide-eyed at my heart's desire, then lay back on the shingle giggling with glee. Ohmigosh! – BRATZ DOLLS GO LESBO! You couldn't make it up.

And you couldn't make it better either. Cos it was perfect the way it was.

And from then on that was all I could think about; the little girl with the short name who stayed on my mind for the longest time, short and sweet. Kim, *Kim*, KIM! We're not much for wordplay round our way, 'less you wanna get a punch up the bracket pronto, but it was like I floated around in a daze for weeks, just smiling at everyone every time I thought of new stuff about her name.

Like: KIM – sounds like 'him', but better. *KIM* – sounds like 'kin', but better. Kim: the best of both worlds.

Kim: nice without ever being dim, which made me wince to think how many times I'd treated her like she was.

Kim: sounds likes hymn; say it loud and there's music playing, say it soft and it's almost like praying.

Kim, so pretty and so plain. So painfully plain to me now – that I loved her. And I'd lost her.

And I had to find her.

As I lay there on the beach I realized that I had two choices in my life, and that if I didn't choose the right one then I wouldn't have a lot of my life left. I could mope around in the shallow end, letting the sea of circumstance wash all around me till I was so smoothed out I had no rough edges left to bash my way to a better life. Or I could make something happen; I could find Stella and beg or bully her to put me in contact with Kim. Shouldn't be that difficult; no disrespect, but at the end of the day she was a right old slapper and would never knowingly prevent a shag, even if her own daughter was the shagee.

But before I went wherever the hunt for Kim might take me, I wanted to say a proper goodbye to Asif. He replied straight away to my text, saying he'd like very much to see me but he was busy at Pride the day I'd suggested. Asif at Pride – this I had to see. At first, being surrounded by more than 100,000 snogging same-sex couples was something I certainly wasn't looking forward to in my current sapphic sulk. But you can't beat 'em, the Brighton gayers, for that one weekend, so you might as well join 'em. When I was but a chav – in the original meaning of the word, a little child – in 1992, Brighton Pride began with only a fistful, only about a hundred, of gaylords blowing, bending and buggering about at their own convenience. Fifteen years later, it's so much part of the mainstream that my little sisters' school spends ages in the run-up making costumes to parade in! I don't know how the gayers can moan about what a homophobic straight society we live in, frankly, when you've got schools actively encouraging ten-year-olds to do projects celebrating a man's right to take it up the wrong 'un!

I turned up at Preston Park with half a bottle of Smirnoff clutched in my clammy paw, and among the hoards waiting for the parade on that steaming Saturday there he was – the least likely person to find at a gay-fest.

Among a group of sweet-faced people holding disapproving placards, the sweetest face of all was one I'd kissed many times.

'Asif!'

He stared at me from behind two hand-written signs, one in each fist, which read JESUS WOULDN'T DO IT! and FISHERS OF MEN – BUT NOT LIKE THAT! Trust Asif to take on the world without ever cussing anyone! 'MARIA!'

I ran up to him, threw my arms around his neck and kissed his lovely lips as the disapproving banners looked down their noses at us. All around us a chorus of tutting broke out. I laughed, looking round at them. 'Jeez, have some patience – I'll get around to all of you in the end!' I laughed again in delight, just for him, holding his lovely face in my hands. 'What are you DOING here?'

In reply he smiled shyly and shook the JESUS WOULDN'T DO IT! banner. 'Oh! – of course. The Christian thing.'

'Come join us in Jesus, sister,' a nice-looking blonde lady suggested.

'I don't think Jesus would have me, to be honest,' I answered, not altogether unregretfully. It seemed like a nice simple life, all black and white and no baffling grey bits. 'But thanks for asking.' I held Asif's hands in mine and stood back to get a last good look at him. 'Well – fight the good fight then.'

'I will,' he said solemnly. 'And in your way, I know you will too, Maria.'

I kissed him one more time, for luck and for almost-love. And that was the last I saw of him – still so beautiful, so good, so lost to me forever.

26

As I turned my back for the last time on my beautiful dark-eyed boy and headed into the park, my mood had already started to lift; partly cos of the vodka, partly from that last lingering kiss, but mostly cos it just felt so good to know what it was I wanted. Some girl was gonna fall head over arse in love with Asif one day (getting the benefit of his Sugar-education!), but it was never going to be me. Now that was sorted it was just the future I had to worry about. And yeah, I'd just been moaning that mine was looking kinda grey rather than a glowing orange, but as I weaved my way deeper into the crowd it was hard not to catch the mood and feel like the world was full of promise after all.

A girl wearing nothing but a fishnet bodysuit, long satin gloves and biker boots asked if I'd take a picture of her and her girlfriend, a pigtailed blonde wearing a neon-pink T and lime-green knickers. I had a jealous moment as the loved-up couple grinned and groped for the camera, but I told myself that once I found Kizza all this could be ours, as I wandered through the laughing and loving and let the party vibe ripple through me.

I finished my half-bottle of vod and clambered up on to one of the fairground rides that were set up round the edge of the park. True, without Kim I felt I was on the outside looking in, but the view was a bloody good one! It was a hot day, which meant there was naked flesh on show all over the park. Screw it – might as well join 'em I thought, peeling of my top and hurling it into the crowds. Less was definitely more and I could have got shagged twenty times over as I climbed down from the carousel and sauntered over to watch the floats arrive. A cute dark-haired chick in a baseball cap and bright yellow Roxy bikini smiled and offered me her can of beer.

'I love love love it when the parade arrives,' she grinned. 'I never miss it.' She looked as excited as a kid who's just seen Santa and (unlike a kid!) she also looked hot. 'Oh my days! – look at that!' she squealed as a float shaped like a horse with a rainbow tail and mane, ridden by knights in white satin carrying enormous swords, came into the park, followed by twenty dancing love hearts.

Foxy Roxy laughed and squealed and I laughed and squealed along with her as we knocked back the beers and cheered on the parade. The floats were coming into Preston Park thick and fast now; there were the good (Amnesty International Pink Tank, Gay Police Association), the bad (all those who'd come purely looking for a shag, if you were morally inclined) and the ugly (the drag queens – let's not bother mincing words). Then there were the funny buggers:

GREEN GAYS SAY RECYCLE YOUR RUBBER

BEARS WITH SORE HEADS

UP TO THE ELBOW BUT PROUD

TORY LEZZERS SAY GET ON YOUR DYKES!

GAY MUSLIMS SAY STOP OCCUPYING SODOM

FASHION AGAINST FASCISM

It was turning out to be a pretty good afternoon after all, I thought, as Roxy decided her beer was better fed to me from her lips rather than from the can. Then among all the fun and games I saw a sight that filled me with all the right-eous anger of a pack of Bible-bashers with PMT being confronted with a gay gang bang behind a bush when they were leading a Sunday school nature study group.

'Oh my days it's THEM! I LOOOVE them! I was SOOO upset when they got attacked, but see, that's the thing about the gay community, we refuse to be victims . . .'

I looked up from where I'd been staring (her cleavage) to see what Foxy was banging on about and there, dressed like twin Elton Johns in that mad get-up he wore for his fiftieth birthday party, all ten-foot wig and white-powdered face and lace, were my two ex-fairy-godfathers, Aggy & Baggy – literally standing on pedestals which, I reflected sourly, looked more like cake stands. Across the front of their float in huge silver letters was written 'TIME TO TAKE OUT THE TRASH', and to the immaculate sound of Franz Ferdinand's 'Take Me Out' a bunch of hyper-sexy teens strutted and swayed, all of them wearing outfits made out of black plastic bin bags.

I stood, gob open, staring at them, and then I realized

that all of them were wearing or holding something I guess was meant to show their 'white trash' status. So one of the boys was accessorizing with an electronic ankle tag and a natty see-through holdall full of iPods and mobiles, another one was wearing a hat and hairnet that were a silver and sequinned version of the ones worn in Macky's and Burger King – and as one of the girls turned to face me, I saw that her bin-bag outfit was meant to be a school uniform, and strapped to her front was a plug-ugly plastic baby. And in the middle stood Duane Trulocke, wearing nothing but a mock-Burberry yashmak.

You know people, when they're banged to rights, often say stuff like 'I don't know what came over me'? Well, I did. Seventeen years of having people who were far from perfect peer down their stuck-up noses at me just because of my postcode. Seventeen years of putting up with snobs whose sexual habits just a few years ago would have had society dismissing them as trash attempting to feel better about themselves by treating other people like trash, of all the tragic hypocrisies. Seventeen years of being slagged off by people who secretly hated themselves and could only kiss it better by hating someone else – the 'chavs' would do for now. All that came over me, and I knew what it was because I had had to fight the feeling so often. And then what came up to me, as luck would have it, was a cheery bloke pushing a dirty great burger trolley loaded down with yummy chavvy treats like bright red ketchup and bright yellow mustard, full of gorgeous E-numbers. And then technicolour rain, the yellow and the red, coming down over the whole nasty, snobby extravaganza that was the 'TIME TO TAKE OUT THE TRASH' float, as I with a whooping war cry jumped up on to the float, exhibiting the grace of a ballerina and the intent of a young hoody about to do serious damage to private property.

So, yeah, I knew what came over me and they knew what went over them! Not blowing my own trumpet, but that float looked like a proper work of art by the time I'd emptied my squeezies over it – yeah, a Jackson Pollock! (Something else I'd learned from Kim, apart from the sexy stuff.)

Course I was on a roll by now, so I chucked the empties into the audience – which by now was how I was starting to think of the astounded crowd, which you can either call self-delusion or self-esteem, take your pick – and looked around for any more alterations and improvements I could make to the tragic kingdom of Bags and Ags. The big cheeses themselves had come down from their pedestals – how apt! – and were trying to climb down off the float, but sadly the tightness of their breeches hampered them somewhat. With an evil laugh I helped them both out with a dainty foot in the small of each broad, thick-skinned back.

The models, if that's the word you'd use to describe such a ragbag of rent boys and fag hags, were screeching and pushing as they too attempted to alight from the mocking tableau, which until recently they had seemed so proud to be a part of. I decided that maybe it was wearing such unpleasant, badly crafted outfits that was causing them such consternation, so did my bit towards restoring their happiness by ripping at any piece of their rubbish rigs I could grab hold of. I saved a special gift for young Duane the two-faced trick-pony – a nice kick in the nuts, and one to grow on – for last; then curses, over the heads of the crowd I could see my old mates the boys in blue making a beeline for me! I took a bow, leaped off the trashed float and made a run for it.

I'm not sure what happened – I think my heel got stuck in the ground, or I tripped over something, but one minute I'm running gazelle-like through the melee, dodging the crowds and making the fat cops and the even fatter B&A look like the jokers they were. Then the next minute I'm sprawled out flat, spilling out of my bra-top and giving every guy and girl in the park a glimpse of what makes Sugar so sweet. Well, I wasn't too bothered about my unplanned peep show, but I was bothered about the sodding great float that was heading straight my way.

It was big and gorgeous, all done up with shells and loads of shiny blue paper floating about in a way that I guess was meant to look like the sea. And then, like Venus from the waves (I watch TV!), this incredible girl stood up from where she'd been perched on a massive great starfish (white chocolate I'm guessing, probably from Choccywoccy-doodah). She was dressed like some sexed-up mermaid, a shimmering green tail very low on her hips, an emerald-type gem sparkling from the depths of her smooth white stomach. Her long red-blonde hair reached down to her shoulders but thankfully not down far enough to cover her chest, which was naked apart from two of the tiniest, shiniest pink seashells you could imagine.

The float stopped and I scrambled to my feet and looked up at the mermaid's face.

It was Kim . . .

Time stood still, the crowd froze, and it would probably have been one of those perfect movie moments 'cept in the movies the heroine doesn't usually say things like 'Fuck me five ways!'! But that's exactly what I said, and then I started to laugh and I couldn't stop, cos I couldn't believe what I was seeing, I couldn't believe life could be this sweet, and I couldn't believe my little Kizza, the shy girl I'd wanted to be bold, was standing in front of a park full of people, bold as you like, with just a few silky scales and a couple of barnacles between her and a full-frontal. And like a horny sailor trying to pull one of them sirens I'd have happily smashed my ship into a bunch of rocks, or in this case a Pride float, to get to her.

'Oi – Lewis!' I shouted. And my gorgeous girl looked down at me and I knew it was all going to be OK. First she looked shocked, then she tried to look like she couldn't give a toss – but she managed to keep that up for about half a second before she broke into a massive, excited, sexy grin.

'SUGAR! What are you doing here?!'

'Looking for you, DYKE – where else would I find you?'

'Get up here, slapper!' She put her hand down to take hold of mine and just then another great hand slammed on to my shoulder with the full force of the law.

'Maria Sweet, I am arresting you—' Fuck, I'd forgotten all about the sodding police! Then like some underwater kung-fu girl Kizza grabbed a big fork thingy off the confused-looking Neptune dude who was standing behind her and shoved it up against the copper's chest, pushing him backwards on to the floor.

'Get your fucking hands off my girlfriend!' New Scary Kizza screamed at the gobsmacked sucker as he landed on his fat arse. Then over her head I saw the crowd parting and a purple-faced Aggy and Baggy, accompanied by yet another member of Her Majesty's Constabulary, heading straight towards us.

I grabbed my avenging angel's hand. 'RUN!' I told her – and we did.

And that's how I ended up on the last train out of Brighton with a sleeping Kizza squashed up nice and close against me. We're gonna go and stay with some mates of hers in a faraway land called 'Up North'. And from there – who knows? Kim still wants to go to university, probably in Manchester, and I'm still a dropout with sod all prospects – 'cept maybe now the prospect of being happy. I don't know what I'm gonna do from here, how to get to my balcony in the sun, but when I finally make it, one thing I'm sure of is that Kim's going to be lying on the sun bed next to mine. Well, once she's knocked me up a jug of sangria, rolled me a spliff and rubbed me all over with bronzing oil – natch.

Like I think I might have said before, if the good life's not handed to you on a silver platter, all you can do is hang on like hell and try not to chip your Hard Candy in the process. So I've grabbed my girl and my chance, I'm out of Brighton and heading for the great unknown. And I gotta say, it feels sweet.

JULIE BURCHILL

Two girls, two worlds, one love affair

Fifteen-year-old Kim is horrified when her dad tells her she's got to leave her posh school and go to the infamous Ravendene Comprehensive. How will she survive in this wild and scary teenage jungle?

But then Kim meets gorgeous Maria Sweet – better known as Sugar. Leaving her good-girl past far behind, Kim finds herself falling under Sugar's spell – and asking herself a disturbing question: has she fallen in love with her best friend?

A major Channel 4 TV series

SUZANNE PHILLIPS

'*They want to know why. Why am I here? What happened to you, Chloe Doe?*'

Arrested for prostitution, seventeen-year-old Chloe is incarcerated at the Madeline Parker Institute for Girls. They want her to reform, to move on to something better, but the way she sees it, everyone's job has one or two things about it they don't like and her job isn't so different. Besides, moving on only matters if you care about the future.

Then she meets her counsellor, Dr Dearborn. He might look like The Joker but he's smart, maybe even as smart as Chloe. Perhaps he can get her to remember the tragedy she'd rather forget and persuade her she's someone worth saving.

A selected list of titles available from Macmillan Children's Books

The prices shown below are correct at the time of going to press. However, Macmillan Publishers reserves the right to show new retail prices on covers, which may differ from those previously advertised.

Julie Burchill

Sugar Rush	978-0-330-41583-2	£5.99

Jaclyn Moriarty

Feeling Sorry for Celia	978-0-330-39725-7	£5.99
Finding Cassie Crazy	978-0-330-41803-3	£5.99
Becoming Bindy MacKenzie	978-0-330-43885-8	£5.99

Suzanne Phillips

Miss America	978-0-330-44870-3	£9.99

Rose Wilkins

So Super Starry	978-0-330-42087-9	£5.99
So Super Stylish	978-0-330-43135-8	£5.99
I ♥ Genie – Wishful Thinking	978-0-330-43880-3	£5.99

All Pan Macmillan titles can be ordered from our website, www.panmacmillan.com, or from your local bookshop and are also available by post from:

Bookpost, PO Box 29, Douglas, Isle of Man IM99 1BQ
Credit cards accepted. For details:
Telephone: 01624 677237
Fax: 01624 670923
Email: bookshop@enterprise.net
www.bookpost.co.uk

Free postage and packing in the United Kingdom